THE BELLS OF REDEMPTION

Chris Michaels

CHRIS MICHAELS

CHAPTER ONE

The glint was minimal but not unseen as he walked slowly down the path of god, surrounded by the seats of sinners. All that surrounded him was a life of chaos and he ruled that kingdom like the god which starred down upon him now. As he stopped and looked down below him, he could see the imperfect creases of a unknown number of kneeled sinners before him, know was his time to find some kind of redemption that lay behind him.

"Please god, let it be known that I did what was necessary for a life to continue, to breathe freely. I know I haven't done this before and yet I understand that my soul may not be saved... Hell, you probably wouldn't want to know what I've done. How many souls I've sent your way. I don't even know if this is the way I want it to be. I've always thought that I wouldn't be accepted, the shadows that I've slept within. But I'm ready to change, even if that is possible, only the voice of fate may reveal that" The words slipped out slower than he ever thought they would, he wasn't even sure if they made sense.

He lifted his head and looked upon the glint that had captured his view. It's curvature was something masterful but yet he knew it was time. To leave all that was left behind on that trail of destruction, to find some kind of solace within the chaos. His eyes focused, landing upon the metal object hung at height, such a simple object but all that touched it's coarse entrail knew that only fate would decide their outcome. He stood up and walked up beneath it. He reached up and wrapped his fingers around it, the coarse rope rubbing against his grip. He inhaled and flicked his wrist as a loud sound echoed. The bell had been chimed and now it was fates decision what was next for him. He took a deep breath and then exhaled slowly. "It's your time, hold yourself true to yourself Ronin and the gods will smile upon your soul" he whispered to himself as his words fell upon the cold stone tomb.

CHAPTER TWO

Everything changes and yet it seems to stay the same. No matter how many years pass, it seems like time stops in that definitive moment. The dreams changed and yet they were always there. If it could have been different. There was nothing that could have changed what happened, very much like everything in life. The darkened shadows dancing like a strange macabre scene from a long lost dance. The clattering of the blades as they danced a song of death that sung a chorus of eternal life within one fatal conclusion. No matter how much he tried to justify the ending, nothing changed the path that led him to this point.

He lay there, sweat soaked from another night lost in the wonderland of his internal chaos. He must remember to take deeper breaths. To slow the mind as much as the warm exhaling oxygen that he pushed out into a cool evening. He ran a hand across the bumpy ridge of a scar as old as he could remember. Although, his memory was old, he was still young in age compared to those that had passed before him. He slowed his breath until he found himself upon a plateau of consciousness, clearing his mind of all shadows that lay upon it. He thought back to the breathing exercises he had done after many brutal training sessions. Allowing his mind and body to become one again and for the bruising to swell upon the hot spots on his body where the blows had struck. But he showed no weakness, no sign of defeat as they caught him for every strike he had committed to and found its mark.

He smiled fondly, for those were the times that made him feel alive, he knew his name and that name was the legacy he swore would outlive him. The wanderer, the nomad, the one who found peace within the wilderness regardless of where he stepped. For his feet had travelled many miles, he was never too far away from where he belonged and that was within himself.

"Ronin..... Yes, Ronin, that's my name" he whispered to himself as he focused upon the ceiling, nothing but a blank canvas lay above him. He positioned his hands upon the bed and hauled himself up. Mornings like these, he felt blessed to experience. He turned his head and watched the lightweight curtains billowing with the morning breeze that flowed in from the open doors. The rays of the morning sun flowed through and he smiled as it seemed that no matter how brutal the storm cried it's anger, the sun smothered it's pain like a parent to a child.

He pushed himself forward as he twisted his body around and allowed his feet to hit the floor. The cold touch of the stone flooring never seemed to bother him, especially after the amount of heat that passed through him after nights like that. As he stood up and felt the cool breeze wrap itself around him, he enjoyed its embrace. He stretched out feeling all the muscles upon his back extend and it felt good to be alive once again. He walked forward and brushed his hand upon the lightweight curtain until he passed beside it and stepped out into the world like a rebirth of a brave new world.

Although he was only dressed in a pair of shorts, the morning glow felt as though he was fully dressed. He loved the early mornings, the feel of it's embrace, the sun rising above the broken horizon with clouds that lined it's very limits sitting upon an ocean so vast, he often wondered where it ended and the sky began. He loved living by the ocean, every morning the ritual would begin again and at that very moment, he would find his reason to live again. The sound of the ocean, breaking upon the shore always calmed him more than he could ever imagine. It was a lost song of the ages, a harmony of the deep and its lyrics were only known by those that held its secret tight within their soul.

"Emiko….." The name swirled around his mind, "Ah yes, the name that evokes a thousand thoughts and yet she will always be next to me wherever I roam upon this world" Ronin thought as he stared out upon the horizon. After all the chaos had ascended upon them and then disbanded like the morning fog being burned out by the rays of the sun, they went their separate ways. Ronin thought back to the last thing he had said to her "All I can say is that we'll go our separate ways and we will meet again where the two bells toll, until then you take care of yourself Emiko and I'll always have your back"

For he knew the location, but the journey would be difficult but that's life wrapped up in its simplest form. So far Ronin had only ever known death and violence. How can a man like himself find the true form of solace and redemption for the darkness he has brought down upon those around. Not just his enemies but also those he loved. These are the questions that he seemed to find unanswerable in some way or another. This is what kept him awake at night, he seemed to always be seeking for answers but nothing came. No matter how much he pondered, meditated or scribbled down his thoughts. "Maybe this is just the way it is" Ronin thought as his concentration broke like a wave upon the glassy sea beneath him. It was time to get some work done, time to work on his craft. "All that I am is ahead of me and all I will be, is within me" Ronin whispered to himself as he stood upright, turned and walked back into the room. It was time to return back to that place that he always considered home and yet he had left many times to find a new place to reside in this world only to return back. Knowing that a piece of his soul was left out there every time he stepped forward into the darkness to find a level of light that would bring a small measure of peace.

CHAPTER THREE

He hadn't noticed at first, maybe it was the thoughts lingering which distracted his concentration, he wasn't sure but the glow in the corner of his eye which brought him back fully to the task in hand. He reached over and picked up his phone, tapped on the screen and saw the green notification appear. It wasn't as much the notification itself, but the name that appeared that made him stop for one moment. He could feel his whole body ready to react, a tense feeling flowed through his body, almost a anxious moment. A florid of emotions began to build within his thoughts, everything from "Why now?" to "Damn, what's happened" Elation to worse case scenario and everything in between began to formulate within his head. But he wouldn't make a conclusion till at least he read what was written. Just the name of Emiko set his mind on fire, she was the only person who had made him feel this way and yet he loved her more than life itself.

He calmed his breathing down to stop his mind running overtime "Maybe, it's all the emotions from last time" Ronin thought as he began to run through some box breathing exercises. Four seconds inhale, hold and release. He did this several times and he began to feel himself slow down and more relaxed. He pressed the screen on his phone and selected the message notification. He found himself holding his breath slightly and started to read, he released a long breath of air as a wave of relief washed over him. Everything was good, he reread the message again

"Hey Benji" Ronin let out a laugh as Emiko always called him that when she wanted to wind him up when they were younger. Even though she accepted his adopted name, he guessed there was a part of her that wouldn't forget where they came from, he read on. "I know it's been some time, maybe for the better considering what happened, enough time has passed and no matter what happened, it's time to move forward. We can't hold the past against us, it is what it is. Let's meet up and I've also got a job I want you to help me with. Don't worry, nothing like the last time we met. I just need your opinion on some antiques I've been given by an old friend. He said that the right person would know their history and also their hidden meaning. Let me know what you think, speak soon!"

With that, Ronin closed down his phone and lay back pondering over the message. A flow of questions poured through his mind, especially the part about the hidden meaning. He did wonder why Emiko thought that he would know, he did have quite an in-depth knowledge of Japanese weaponry, so that was the only reason he could think of why she had messaged him. All these years had passed, he no longer needed to bodyguard after he received a large sum of money from Sato for saving his life. He had explained to Ronin not long after that night what had happened. After realising that the inevitable was going to happen, Sato had escaped and with a few loyal men, they made their way away from the house to put as much distance as possible between himself and Tanaka, ending in a safe house not far that Sato had acquired for this very reason. He had known it would have been good hunting for Tanaka and his men. He had felt nothing but sympathy towards the man who was once one of his closest friends and also Ronin's father. He had wondered how anyone could become so corrupt and twisted through greed, a complete dishonour upon himself and his entire family.

He pondered for quite a while before deciding what to do next. It wasn't that he didn't want to see her but he had always stood back a distance from her for fear of wanting to keep close to her to protect her. He had made his mind up, even though he had spent so many times wondering how he would react when he saw her again. He tapped the screen and pressed the message app icon, he started to write the message out but then deleted it several times before leaving it as it was. It simply read 'I'll meet you where the two bells toll two days from now at midday' and pressed send. He lay the phone down on the small coffee table before repositioning himself and continuing his meditation session. So many thoughts flowed through him, he often spent anything up to 30 minutes a day in complete silence, allowing his mind to clear itself of all the thoughts that filled his mind. He found that he could lower his breathing to a point where he took himself into a trance. It was as if he had transported himself to a different plane of thinking. He had spent years studying the way of Zen Buddhism, like his ancestors before him. It allowed him to peak in his training, taking him to a place of Mushin or 'No Mind' a place where no thoughts came or went. A void within his mind, not even the single wisp of air could be heard moving past his head. As he sat there, especially in a posture that most would find uncomfortable. This kneeling position known as Seiza, which allowed him to place his palms down upon his slightly opened thighs, keeping himself centred at all times.

Throughout this time of silence, he would often lift his hands up and recreate the ancient Kuji Kiri also known as the nine hand seals or cuts, whilst softly repeating the Kuji In or the nine mantras. So often he found himself, almost religiously moving his hands at a pace that flowed with each other, working together. Everything from Rin (Power) to Jin (Awareness) and then ending with Zen (absolute) as well as its associated mantra of "I am the void and the light" after several renditions of these, he allowed his mind to resurface to a plateau that was purged of all unwanted thoughts. He had perfect clarity and focus, he knew what needed to be done and so it shall be. With that, Ronin took one final exhale and allowed himself to awaken from his spiritual self and return to his physical self. It was time to prepare himself for his encounter with fate. And with that, he rocked forward before flexing himself to rise and allow his body to readjust. It was time to begin his own journey of a thousand miles, return back to a place that he had been lost to but also a place where he had found himself and today was going to be a good day.

CHAPTER FOUR

The birdsong that surrounded him, calmed his ever beating heart, even though he had prepared and cleared his mind a hundred times, Ronin slowed his breathing to a calming pace. Stood before him in this magnificent arena of space and time lay two of the last relics of a lost generation. Two temples, identical to each other stood separated by a large Japanese garden filled with many incredible sights. Traditional Japanese gardens can be categorised into three types: tsukiyama (hill gardens), karesansui (dry gardens) and chaniwa gardens (tea gardens). The main purpose of any Japanese garden is to attempt to be a space that captures the natural beauties of nature, and clearly this one certainly did that. Ronin felt privileged to be standing here, between these two incredible temples and an exquisite space between them, Japanese gardens are believed to originated around the 7th century. This particular garden was modelled upon the Joruri-ji Garden in Nara which is located in the Japanese countryside, not far from Osaka. The Joruri-ji garden is extremely peaceful and isolated. It was built in 1047, and is an incredible example of the 'paradise garden'. The pond in the middle symbolises the ocean between birth and death. The nine Buddha statues represent the nine stages of nirvana.

Nirvana is the final stage of the noble eightfold path which includes: right view, right aspiration, right speech, right action, right livelihood, right effort, right mindfulness, right concentration.

Ronin found himself drifting back in time to when he found himself being sat in front of his sensei being told the tale of the eightfold path and what it meant to walk it. The ancient path of life and death, of birth and the continuation of life through the conscious connections of the senses. The origins of the conscious mind coupled with the body and the spirit. These truths he learned from an early age and something that stayed deep within his mind. Learning this path to true nirvana and the realisation of Samsara.

He stood and looked across, not just at this incredible garden but far beyond that. Where he stood he could see valleys and the rolling hills in the distance. But to him, this was one and the same, all part of the beauty that made this place a homestead to the generations that came before him. The temples and the garden before became the attachment that he searched for deep within him. Ronin had learnt the art of detachment for specific areas in his life but being stood here brought it all back to him and the last words he spoke to Emiko. The time was now and here in this place was the moment everything changed. He had stood and wondered why the bells created such memories for him. The two bells that faced each other were known as Bonshō but also known as tsurigane or ōgane. These large bronze bells were typically found within Buddhist temples and used to summon the monks to prayer as well as demarcate periods of time. The difference between these bells and normal bells were that they were struck on the outside with either a handheld mallet or a beam suspended on ropes.

Not only did they have a significance of indicating time but also a spiritual connection. They played a an important role within Buddhist ceremonies, especially at New Year and Bon festivals. But more than that, the Bonshō bell became a symbol of world peace. Something that Ronin had wished within his lifetime but knew it would not be possible whilst there was corrupt and violent minds with cruel intentions still living. He had seen his fair share of violence and it was something that he avoided at all costs but knew it was necessary to attain the peace he required. He had accepted that violence was something that he was particularly skilled in but not proud of. He turned his head away from the bells. "Why does being here make it so difficult yet so plain to see that I carry the guilt of death upon my soul?" Ronin thought as he cleared his mind and thoughts. Just being back here always does this to him. He had a task to carry out and one that was the path he needed to walk. As he brought his vision back upon the garden, he saw something or rather someone standing there. He wondered how he had missed it. But as soon as he saw the outline of the person, he knew who it was and smiled.

Before he could make a move, a voice rang out. "Are you not coming to greet me brother? We are between these two great bells and yet we make more noise than these two have in their lifetime" Ronin laughed to himself as Emiko still spoke in riddles after all these years. He stepped forward and made his way towards her. As he came closer, he could see that age had not affected her and she was as fresh as the last time they were together. Ronin broke out a smile and spoke "I see time has escaped you once again sister and yet you still speak in a tongue that could confuse the gods" he said as she gave him a look only a brother could appreciate as one would.

CHAPTER FIVE

"So what's next?" Asked Ronin as he stood in front of the only person who he felt connected to and yet he was always so far away from. Emiko stood and looked directly at Ronin, wondering if he could sense the anxiety that flowed throughout her. It had seemed like yesterday that she stood next to him on that night that changed everything, as she stepped back closer into the shadows and away from Ronin and the fallen Tanaka. Fate had definitely found him that night and yet in that very moment everything had changed. She pondered upon her answer as she thought long and hard but in this very moment she knew that only the truth would suffice.

She inhaled deeply and then exhaled, allowing the breath to disperse into the air. "As I said, I have some antiques that I have obtained that I want your opinion on. They are exactly within your remit and area of expertise" Emiko explained as she opened the bag that was sling over her shoulder. She slid her hand into it and pulled out an object that was wrapped within a cloth. It looked heavy by the way that Emiko held it. Ronin looked on patiently whilst she held the object out in front of her beckoning for Ronin to take it. He reached out and removed it from Emiko's hand, it was heavy but there was something different about it. As he started to unfold the cloth that was wrapped around it. As soon as he had pulled over the cloth, he saw a glint of silver, he was intrigued. After opening it fully, his eyes widened. As soon as he saw the metallic object in its pure beauty, he couldn't believe what was within his grasp.

The divine shape and curvature of the metal was impeccable, polished to a mirror even after all these years. What Ronin held in his hand was literally a piece of history that had shaped a nation. It was a Tsuba, a hand guard from a Japanese samurai sword or otherwise known as a katana, but this was not just any Tsuba. It belonged to the one of the most famous of all samurai clans, the 'Tokugawa Clan'

If you know, you know. It's intricate design and shape was known as a 'mon' or the 'Triple Hollyhock' although it is commonly, but mistakenly identified as 'Hollyhock', the 'aoi' actually belonged to the Birthwort family and translates as 'Wild Ginger' (Asarum) It has been a readily recognised icon in Japan, it symbolises in equal parts, both as the Tokugawa clan as well as the last shogunate.

But there was something different to this Tsuba,

around the edging that Ronin could see were Japanese symbols engraved, he wasn't sure which style it was as there three different types, these are kanji, hiragana, and katakana. But what he did know was that this was old. He put his hand in his pocket for a moment and took out his phone. He thought if he could at least get a photo of it, then he may be able to get an understanding of potentially what was written. As he held his hand as still as possible, with the other he aligned the camera and set the camera to take a photo after 3 seconds. As this was done, he pressed on the photo and zoomed in. He stopped and looked up at Emiko and then back down at the Tsuba. If he was correct in his thinking, what he held in his hand wasn't just any Tsuba. It belonged to one of Japan's greatest samurai and ninja. No sword had ever been found that belonged to him and even though myths had been circulated that he was indeed a master sword smith, these were false. What was true though was that he was in fact a master swordsman. Possibly only comparable to Miyamoto Musashi. The greatest swordsman that ever lived, it is thought that he was undefeated through 60 duels, although many argue that he lost to Musō Gonnosuke.

Ronin looked again and then up at Emiko, he said very slowly and calmly "If this is the real thing, then what I hold in my hand is one the greatest mysteries ever to exist, do you think this is what we believe it to be?" Emiko looked at Ronin and explained "I believe so, there's been so many rumours regarding this and yet no actual facts that back them up, until now. If this is what it is, then what you're holding is a piece of unsolved Japanese history that's priceless. Nothing like this has ever been discovered but yet, people have searched for centuries for this piece"

Ronin looked down at the object again and then back at his phone. What he could make out of the symbols themselves were 服部 半蔵 roughly translated to **Hattori Hanzō** or otherwise known as his nickname Oni no Hanzō 'Demon Hanzō'

Hanzō was a famous ninja of the Sengoku era, he served the Tokugawa clan as a samurai and was credited with saving the life of Tokugawa Leyasu and helping him to become the ruler of a united Japan.

There had been rumours of the lost sword of Hanzō circulating for centuries, the sword he used to assist Leyasu in uniting Japan. But as all good tales, it was exactly that, a myth. Or until now if Ronin thought correctly. It was also said that whoever held the sword was blessed with immortality as no known record of Hanzō's death was actually recorded and found. It was almost comparable to the ancient myths of 'Excalibur' But firstly, they would have to get the symbology clarified and that meant contacting only one person that Ronin knew would help him discover the truth. That meant travelling to Japan itself, to the very heart of Hamzō's realm and find the hidden truth.

CHAPTER SIX

J apan is a fascinating country, one that's steeped in history and traditions. A place that's one of the most advanced technological countries in the world built from the ashes of the old Japan and warfare but also one that's locked in ancient traditions, wary and fearful of outsiders and external influences. Haneda Airport lay within the harbour of Tokyo Bay, the same place on July 8, 1853, American Commodore Matthew Perry led his four ships into, seeking to re-establish for the first time in over 200 years regular trade and discourse between Japan and the western world.

Ronin was never a fan of flying, especially long haul. But it allowed him to gain time to concentrate on researching as much as he could on not only Hanzō but anything that could give him a true understanding of the origins of the Tsuba and its connection to the Tokugawa Clan or shogunate. That was the other part of Japanese history, there were literally hundreds of family connections and names to scroll through, especially being one of the most turbulent times in its histories.

Even when Ronin started his search on Tokugawa Leyasu he found reams of information. Everything from a Wikipedia search to the obscure sites. He knew as much that he was roughly born in January of 1543 under the name of Matsudaira Takechiyo and was the founder and first Shōgun of the Tokugawa Shogunate of Japan, which ruled Japan from 1603 until the Meiji Restoration in 1868. He was one of the three 'Great Unifiers' of Japan, along with his former lord Oda Nobunaga and Toyotomi Hideyoshi. But to find any leads to the exact search of the potential roots of the possibilities that the sword of Hanzō actually existed. That until now was just the imagination of Hollywood especially with movies such as 'Kill Bill' but he needed more than just fictional information, he needed facts. He knew one place that may be the best place to start and that was known as simply the Japanese Sword Museum in Sumida City, not far from the centre of Tokyo itself. Although Emiko had suggested travelling with him, Ronin explained that she stay back and use the resources she had through the family connection. Japanese businessmen spend a lot of time socialising within small circles, often within secret but also within families. Every noble family throughout Japanese history had some connection or another.

Ronin knew that no matter what happened in the next few hours, he would do whatever it took to unlock a mystery the world has never understood. Very much as mysterious as Hanzō's death itself. Ronin had questioned the statement as soon as he read it. He had pondered over it many times and couldn't believe that anyone had not asked the same question as he had "What actually happened to Hanzō?" Although in one version it states that he died in at the age of 54 in 1596. Coming from two theories, one of them states that he was assassinated by a rival ninja, the pirate Fūma Kotarō in which Hanzō had tracked him down to the Inland Sea, Kotarō lured him and his men into a small channel and used oil to set the channel on fire. The other theory is that Hanzō became a monk in Edo where he lived out the rest of his days until he died of illness. So which one to believe? If Ronin was to go off the second one, then Hanzō never died at 54 in 1596, he could have quite possibly live a long and fruitful life way into 1600, leaving the life of chaos and death far behind him, explaining why if he had kept his own katana with him, simply of a reminder of the life he left behind and then broken upon his death by his own wishes, that it had never been found. Ronin knew Japan well, especially Tokyo and the surrounding area. But as stated in the second theory, it says Edo. Well Edo was indeed better known as Tokyo.

Ronin knew the history well, having been taught it as a child. He recalled the lessons he had taught and knew very well that the history of Tokyo goes back some 400 years. As he was told that originally it was named Edo and that it had started to flourish after Tokugawa Ieyasu established the Tokugawa Shogunate in 1603. Edo was the center of politics and culture in Japan, it had grown into a huge city with a population of over a million by the mid-eighteenth century. Throughout this time, the Emperor resided in Kyoto, which was the formal capital of the nation. The Edo Period in which it took its name lasted for nearly 260 years until the Meiji Restoration in 1868, when the Tokugawa Shogunate ended and imperial rule was restored. The Emperor moved to Edo, which was renamed Tokyo. Thus, Tokyo became the capital of Japan.

As Ronin made his way to the museum after landing and clearing customs, his mind was whirling with so many different prospects. He had an understanding of Hanzō was the foundation of all of Japan's successes in one way or another. He was the legendary Ninja and Samurai that helped shape the country for what it is today. The part that he was trying to formulate and bring together was which theory would he believe? With any theory there was always going to be multiple variables involved. If he simply accepted that Hanzō had been assassinated as many suggested, then how was it that he had that Tsuba in his possession? Wouldn't they have stripped him of his sword and passed along various generations? So many questions and not enough time. He decided that it was better to at least to get an opinion on it and take it from there. He knew from extensive research that the museum was run by Nihon Bijutsu Token Hozon Kyokai (The Society for Preservation of Japanese Art Swords) a public interest incorporated foundation established in February 1948 to preserve and promote Japanese swords that have artistic value. It's Chairman and Representative Director was Tadahisa Sakai. That very name was distinctive to Japanese history as well as modern video games, especially within the gaming community that had played 'Ghost of Tsushima'. Ronin recalled remembering reading a document regarding the Sakai Clan. It seems that around 150 years ago, at the end of Japan's Edo period, there was a rebel clan of samurai chose mass suicide after refusing to end their samurai lifestyle. But in the remote, mountainous Shonai region, there was the Sakai clan of samurai, they opted for a dignified surrender. They gave up their swords and destroyed their castle, they created a regional bank as well as a silk farming industry, and then threw their support behind the new Meiji government.

Even though sixteen generations have passed since that first feudal Sakai clan leader presided over Shonai, their legacy lives on through Tadahisa Sakai. At 71, the locals refer to him as the last descendant of the Sakai Clan. He is a revered man in the Shonai region. Even though Sakai is the curator of the Chido museum in Yamagata prefecture which was founded in 1950 by one of his ancestors, he created the Japanese sword museum to preserve Art Swords that were used for rituals or religious facilities.

This was a pretty impressive resume Ronin thought when he had been researching potential leads to connect with. Even from the first contact with Sakai-San who expressed genuine interest when discovering the possibilities of where this could lead to, especially as his own family had served the Tokugawa Clan.

CHAPTER SEVEN

The Japanese Sword Museum was located on the banks of the Sumida River, overlooking the former Yasuda Garden. All though there is much uncertainty about its origins, it's believed to have been built from 1688 to 1703 by Lord Honjo Inabanokami Munesuke, younger brother of Kensho-in, mother of the fifth Tokugawa Shogun Tsunayoshi. Even though it had been remodelled over the years, it was still quite stunning as Ronin looked upon it with awe. If the meeting went well, maybe there may be some truth to the rumours. Ronin had even started to think that maybe Sakai had some inner family knowledge himself regarding Honzō and the mystery that had befallen upon him.

Overlooking Yasuda Garden invoked a lot of memories for Ronin, especially all that occurred with the last encounter. He had done everything he could to resolve the situation as peacefully as possible. But he knew that fate would intervene and to face off against Tanaka, he knew that his destiny had been spoken. His skills had been tested to the limit in that fateful duel. He had given Tanaka a chance to back down but that was never going to something that was written in Tanaka's vocabulary. Destiny and fate have a way of being fulfilled in ways in which the gods could never truly be spoken. To look into his father's eyes for that last moment, all that he was, would be determination in destiny's hand that had been drawn. It had taken a heavy toll upon him, he had spent hours meditating, looking for the answers he required. He often thought that the redemption he was looking for may never be found. For that was the last part of a puzzle that had been built by the pieces that were placed within the tapestry of a life he had built through the taking of life. That was all that he had known for the majority of his life, but now, he wanted forgiveness. From who, he had no answers to that.

With this new discovery that could change, especially after his conversions with Sakai-San which had been quite revealing. Honzō had been the missing piece of this puzzle that linked Sakai-San's family and Tokugawa. Even though Sakai-San's and Honzō had served Tokugawa, Saikai-San's family had spent several months after Tokugawa's rise to the shogunate with Hozō. Much conversation had been had between them. Ronin had wondered what that conversation had been and did they have any answers to his disappearance, whether that's his actual death or the life he lived as a monk.

Ronin checked his watch and decided it was time to get to the meeting with Sakai-San, whatever fate was written was going to be the way it would be. He turned away from the garden and made his way to the museum entrance in which an appointment had been made for him. He was a few minutes early, but that was the way he had always done things. As he approached the entrance, Ronin had started to feel the anxiety build, but with simple breathing exercises, he calmed his breathing down and started to relax.

The entrance was shaped as though it was a face with two eyes above a piece of concrete that shaded the entrance, which was centred in the building. He could see a man standing there waiting for him, as he approached, the security guard as Ronin worked it out started to unlock the door to open it for him. Ronin looked at him and brought himself to bow as was expected "Kon'nichiwa, o ai dekite kōeidesu. Sakai-san ni ai ni kimashita" (hello, pleasure to meet you. I'm here to meet Sakai-San) The security guard looked at Ronin and returned the bow before replying "Kon'nichiwa Beirī-san tōken hakubutsukan e yōkoso. Sakai-san ga omachi shite orimasu. Ko no yō ni kite kudasai" (Hello Bailey-San, welcome to the Japanese sword museum. Sakai-San is waiting for you. Please come this way) Ronin smiled and followed him. Ronin was impressed with the internal decor, lights that flowered like bouquets on the ceiling. Circles decorated the floor and the cool contemporary colours complemented the walls and ceiling. Bouquets of colourful flowers were positioned on stands against the wall. This modern design of glass, steel and lights made it peaceful considering some of the incredible weapons housed within. It was silent as they made their way through the entrance and along a corridor, only their feet making gentle taps as they made their way past several sets of Samurai armour, until they got to a large room. As they came to the entrance, Ronin could see another man, smartly dressed and looking very healthy for his age. This could be the man that unlocks the very mystery that Ronin held in his possession.

As Sakai-San turned around and smiled, he gave a formal bow and answered "Ohayō beirī-san, ogenkidesuka?" (Good morning Bailey-San, I hope you are well?) Ronin returned the formality and replied "Ohayō Sakai-san, arigatōgozaimashita. Yoroshikuonegaishimasu" (Good morning Sakai-San, I am very well thank you. It is an honour working with you) With the formalities conducted Sakai-San spoke first, his voice clear and calculated, thoughtful and insightful "It is an honour for you to be here Bailey-San, now I'm sure you're well versed in Japanese, but let us speak openly in English, wouldn't you agree?" Sakai-San asked. Ronin paused for a moment, impressed with Sakai-San's ability to switch languages so fluent and with ease. Ronin have a slight chuckle and replied "Yes Sakai-San let's do, it's good that we can converse in both Japanese and English, now let's not waste any time, as we discussed, this piece may unlock many answers but also a multitude of questions. I'm sure you're own family history is familiar with the legacy of Hanzō and that no actual sword was ever discovered, well until potentially now and that the ending of his life is a bit of a mystery. I've researched as much as I can and all I do is hit dead ends. If this Tsuba is indeed Hanzō's then this will unlock a lot as there will be the remaining pieces out there somewhere. According to legend, this sword when pieced together, it gave the handler a power beyond imagination. Now that may well be almost the same as the legacy of Excalibur and that was pure energy from lay lines transferred through the sword or this is what was meant to be. You've seen the photos, maybe it's best to place this here and I'm fascinated in hearing your own perspective and thoughts?" Ronin answered whilst placing the Tsuba in front of him upon a glass topped table.

CHAPTER EIGHT

Sakai spent several minutes in complete silence, walking around the table and then stopping and bending down further. This was before he had even picked up the Tsuba, it was as if he was picking up on a strange aura given off by it. He finally reached out and placed his hand over it, he looked at Ronin and smiled "I do believe this indeed has a resonance that is eons old and may well be at one point in its life been attached to the very sword used by Hanzō to help Tokugawa reach Shogun. Its vibrations are strange though, there is a lot known about Hanzō but also so much that is never known. Even his own linage is known to have faded and even his own sons did not live up to their father's legendary status. We can discuss all that later though. For now though, I can wholeheartedly agree that this indeed could well be part of one of the legendary 'Hanzō' swords which hundreds have claimed to hold and even then, they have no real substance in their claims. I know I don't need to even pick this up yet as I can feel the deep vibes that it's giving off. It's strange, it's as though it's searching for its master, or maybe to be joined back with its other pieces. For hundreds of years, there has been a rumour that after Hanzō's death, his favourite sword was broken into several pieces and scattered across Japan in several locations. Now I'm not saying that I completely agree with the rumours, especially with the claims that once the pieces once rejoined can give its owner true shinobi skills. What is meant by that I believe is just that, rumours. Also, that it's value is potentially within the millions, which is exactly another reason why there's a lot of people searching for it for their own personal gain" Sakai said whilst turning his head down and giving a sigh.

Ronin wasn't quite sure what to say, he stood waiting to see what Sakai was going to say. But one thing he knew was that he was in the right place as well with the right person, if he was going to get an answer. He had so many questions he wanted to ask. He stood there milling in his mind the research he had done previously. So he decided that he would fire a couple of quick questions at Sakai first. To see what his reaction would be. Ronin knew that if he had any knowledge that he wasn't sharing with him, then he would know. He was looking at Sakai who was still standing still looking at the Tsuba. "Sakai-san, I know that there are several rumours regarding Hanzō's death, according to the official report, he died in 1596 and that his band of ninjas were said to have died with him. But not physically, but that they disinterested the less able management and that their discipline and training began to slack. I also know that Hanzō's remains are meant to be kept at Sainen-ji temple cemetery, apparently surrounded by his favourite battle spear and helmet. But what I don't understand is how do we know this if no one actually knows he died when it's speculated and is it actually Hanzō in that grave?" Ronin said looking directly at Sakai waiting for an answer. Sakai said nothing at first but looked at Ronin, smiled and simply said "Ronin-san, if we're meant to believe all is written then why are we questioning the authenticity of this Tsuba?"

Ronin wasn't sure what to say next as what Sakai had said was actually very truthful. He knew that Hanzō had sons and it was said that they did not gain the abilities as well as their father. Before he could think anything else, Sakai stopped and lowered his head closer to the Tsuba. It was if he had seen something that was capturing his view. He turned his head several times and picked up a magnifying glass that was placed on the edge of the glass table. As he looked through it intensely and then raised his head and looked at Ronin. Without a moment to lose, Sakai said "Bailey-san, can I ask you what Hanzō's nickname was?"

Ronin took one look and simply replied "Oni no Hanzo or Hanzō the Demon"

Sakai smiled and said "So why does this Tsuba have

the symbol for Demon or Akuma engraved on it?"

Ronin couldn't believe his luck, maybe this was actually the sword that was rumoured to be never made. And if so, how did it ever surface after all these years. So many questions were filling his mind. He had to make a decision of what's next. Before he could ask anymore questions, Sakai asked "So I have no doubt that this was potentially part of the lost sword or one of his swords, what I'm trying to work out is where the rest of it is. There are some strange engraving on it and if it is part of his actual sword, we can't allow this to be known. Especially with the rumours I've heard" before Sakai could continue, Ronin interjected "What do you mean Sakai-san? What rumours are those?" Sakai looked like he had just released the worlds greatest secret. He looked away for a moment and then looked back at Ronin.

"Well, according to some legends, the demon or devil that's cast upon steel can unlock a chamber that holds the true path of the spirit of Hanzō. But they are fantastical stories, created to make it sound as though he was more than human. The other part is that his true self would show itself again once the one that wanders the land brings his soul back to life when the pieces are reunited" Sakai said. Silence fell for a few good moments. Both men stood looking at the Tsuba. Finally the silence was broken by Sakai. "Come Bailey-san, let's get some refreshments, enough has been discovered here today. You can take the Tsuba and we'll discuss this in more depth, I have a few scrolls that you would be interested in looking at" he said, looking like a child who had won first prize before walking slowly off. Ronin reached over and scooped up the Tsuba and wrapped it back up quickly before following Sakai along the corridor.

Ronin was seated opposite Sakai, no words had been exchanged between them. They sat silent but observant of each other. Sakai broke the silence "So what's your thoughts Ronin-san? We know as much that this is possibly a Tsuba that belonged to Hanzō, but as you know yourself, history does have a way of changing. You're aware that Hanzō is believed to be buried right here in Tokyo buried with his favourite weapons and that his bloodline was not as strong as himself. But which version of events do we believe? The one that he is buried here or maybe within that cave? So many questions and not enough answers. As for yourself, you're aware that the one that aligns with his true bloodline can unlock Hanzō's history. We know his last bloodline so far settles at Ryuji Hattori. But as history always states that we must take all at face value. Now we must focus our attention on searching for clues to the location of this cave. Do you agree Bailey-san?"

Ronin took a moment to think of what was next. He made his decision quickly "Yes Sakai-san, I think we do need to do more research. We could easily take history as it is and forget it but that still wouldn't explain why that demon engraved on the Tsuba. I don't know if you're aware that there others that have spoken about this before. Some-one I have had the most unfortunate dealings with. Someone who spent years searching for rare Japanese objects, especially anything that is con-nected to samurai history" Ronin said. Sakai shook his head in agreement "Yes Bailey-san, that is very true, can I ask you something, you don't have to answer if you don't" Sakai replied. A moment of si-lence overtook Ronin, regarding if he should give Sakai a true answer. But if he didn't than he knew that would be dishonest.

Ronin breathed deeply "Of course you can Sakai-san" Ronin answered. Sakai was the kind of person who had nothing to hide himself but was inquisi-tive about many things "Was this person we're discussing connected with your late father Kaito Tanaka?"

CHAPTER NINE

Ronin took a few moments before answering, he knew that whatever answer he gave wouldn't change anything. "Yes Sakai-san, he was. My father Tanaka-san dealt with a lot of very persuasive and influential people, usually those that dealt with criminal connections. The person that we're discussing certainly dealt with a lot of the criminal underground especially within Japanese historical weaponry. Now that we know what this potentially has some connections with Hanzō then we've got to keep this between us. Once rumours start spreading, he will certainly be onto us and be after any information we have, usually not with good intentions. He has far reaching connections and it won't end well Sakai-san" Ronin answered. Sakai nodded and answered "Yes you are right, I wouldn't want to get involved with him and keep him as far as possible with any investigation. I shall investigate further with the scrolls I have. There was something interesting with one of them though that I wanted to show you, simply to get your opinion on it" Sakai said. He laid on of the scrolls upon the table and unrolled it, weighing it down with a couple of unused cups.

Sakai began "So we know Hanzō lived and operated within Iga, which we know is Ninja territory. We know that Hanzō was a nickname for his true name of Hattori Masanari, Hattori warriors in Iga were of both Taira and Minamoto lineage, which means that such lineage affiliation was not a factor in the formation of the Hattori led Iga warriors. As there was a special relationship between Tokugawa Ieyasu and the Iga Hattori, you can only guess that although Ieyasu was a Minamoto, he was certainly a practical general who looked at the history of the Iga Hattori, he had the loyalty of Masanari's father, only to conclude that the Iga Hattori were trustworthy. Then, with Masanari's assistance in Ieyasu's escape through Iga solidified this trust, leading Ieyasu to use Iga warriors as a permanent police force within Edo castle grounds. So all the history can get complicated, we know this much, but let's assume for one moment that we already know the Hanzō was a Ninja but serve more generally as a Samurai. Now we also know that with those kind of loyalties to Tokugawa meant that he had free reign of Iga and we also know that Iga itself is covered in Ninja history, old forts and ruins of its past. I think it's time to look over Iga to gain an understanding of its topography and the layout. Now I said I wanted your opinion on something, if you look at this passage which states about the mountain that never sleeps, what symbol does that look like?" Sakai asked as he picked up a toothpick and placed it between two closely printed symbols.

Ronin leant forward, but he would need to look more closely. He picked up the magnifying glass that laid close to the map. He spent a few moments looking before placing the glass back down. He sat back and looked at Sakai. "If I'm not mistaken, that indeed does look like a demon symbol. A little smudged in place mistaking it for an error, well hidden. So that would make it 'Demon Mountain; the mountain that never sleeps' Now that is a mystery in itself, maybe we should look at the Iga map and then decide if we can unlock this. If we're on the search for a cave within or under a mountain that supposedly contains one of the greatest mysteries unknown to man, then we need to get as much information as possible, wouldn't you agree Sakai-san?" Ronin said.

"Yes you are right, I have many questions and I don't want any of them to be lost in the overall understanding of this. If and I say that lightly, if we can even begin to determine where this mountain is located, then the next part is how do we find a potential entrance? And all this without alerting anyone. It is still a task to travel anywhere without anyone noticing your activities, especially within this region. There's a lot of people who still believe in the old tales of dragons and ninja magic. Some of it as you're aware of is quite dark and unpredictable. Right we will have a look at the map of Iga and then call it a day, we don't want to allow all of this to overload us on the first day heh Bailey-san?" Sakai answered.

Ronin grinned and bowed his head down. Sakai moved the cups from the scroll before letting it roll up on itself. He placed it back within a tube and sealed it. He then opened another one and let a roll of paper slide out. As he unrolled it upon, Ronin could see that it was an old map, very old indeed. When fully unrolled, it's texture was indeed old, faded in places and worn, but overall it was complete. Ronin could see plenty of features and Japanese symbology describing or naming particular areas. He was trying to understand what it all meant, that is until Sakai spoke "Here, see here" Sakai said as he pointed to a certain area with a cocktail stick. Ronin leant forward and tried to make out it in detail, he wasn't sure but he thought what he saw there resembled something of a mountain, before he could answer, Sakai spoke again "Ever since our original conversation, I've been spending time looking over this particular map. There has been a rumour passed down throughout my family, this I learned as a child. They led a peaceful life, not following the warrior way but they were entrusted as a close family to Tokugawa. There was apparently a mountain that many whispered it's name but never truly spoken about. It was supposed to lead you to a great revelation, you could discover your true potential. When I heard these whispers, the mountain was simply known as 'Doragonmaunten' or Dragon Mountain. So you can why your story stirred particular interest in it?" Sakai asked. Ronin looked at the map again and then back up at Sakai. "Yes I can see why, do you believe the rumours Sakai-san, do you think the Tsuba is the key to unlocking this mountain?" He asked. Sakai at first didn't answered. He leant back and gave a slight frown. "Well that would be like saying all paths lead to gold eh Bailey-san? Who truly knows, but it would be truly incredible if we could unlock this mystery and end all the rumours" he answered.

CHAPTER TEN

Ronin had decided not to play his hand too quick when it came to making decisions, especially when it came to important ones like this. He had all the potential evidence that he needed, but was missing one part and that was the actual truth of whether the Tsuba he possessed was the one that would unlock it all. His mind was in the ether, wandering through time and space right now on what course of action he should take without his past chasing him down and dragging him back to duel again. His father was dead by his own hands, that's tough for anyone to deal with, but the implications it brought were more far reaching than he could ever imagine. He had truly stepped into the arena when it came to creating enemies. The thought of Nietzsche's famous quote 'Whoever fights monsters should see to it that in the process he does not become a monster. And if you gaze long enough into an abyss, the abyss will gaze back into you' He had certainly almost done that with his last course of action. Daichi Yamada was not the kind of person that you actually wanted to cross paths with, well not unless you did not value your life or family. He was as dangerous as they came. He himself had seen the aftermath of what happened to someone that stepped on his Yamada's toes and it wasn't pleasant. Ronin had in the past had dealings with some of Yamada's associates and yet he wasn't going to return there. The tasks he had been asked to carry out questioned whether he had an actual soul, disposing of certain people without trace of his involvement, to strike like a wraith in the cold dark night. When it came to carrying out the task, someone had seemed to get there first and eliminated the named party with a certain drone strike. To Ronin, he was relieved, not in the sense of that he had lost a business opportunity but because that would have been another strike upon his soul he wouldn't have to deal with later on down the line.

"Is everything ok Bailey-san? You look a million miles away" came the voice. Ronin blinked and refocused on the soft eyes of Sakai, he smiled "Apologies Sakai-san, I was lost in thought for a moment there. Our biggest problem is that we need to make moves that are unknown to Yamada-san, which is nearly impossible due to his far reaching influences and associates, especially within the Iga region. It still has a lot of ears and eyes in place which are hidden in plain sight. If, and I don't say this lightly, if he does get to know what prize is up for grabs, then he will do whatever it takes to claim it and that doesn't rule out murder. So we've definitely got to keep everything under wraps for now. I propose that we work under the pretence that we are carrying out topographical work to understand the natural formations of mountains, we will bring in some archeological experts as well to over compensate for the cover story. Once we start making moves, we have to work quickly. What says you Sakai-san?" Ronin answered. Sakai exhaled and nodded in agreement "Yes Bailey-san, you are right. We can't have anyone knowing the true intentions of what we're searching for. If the location of Hanzō's cave is indeed locked within this dragon mountain, then it wouldn't take long for dangerous forces to turn their hand to crime to get to their prizes. The value of its content would be priceless. I think we better move quickly laying a plan of action and getting all members of this expedition in place. I genuinely think that we need to take our time but get this done like it was yesterday if you get my meaning. I don't need anyone like Yamada-san learning of its true intentions, especially as he has an army of assassins ready to strike. I've heard of his previous business dealings where he sealed a lucrative deal with another businessman, only to then send in his team to wipe him out. Once the deal had been signed, there was nothing the other man could have done. His only cause of action is remove any kind of threats to him losing the prize before it happens. Now let's get to work on this and begin to plan this out"

Sakai said before he rolled the maps back up and sealed them within a tube.

Ronin sat debating on what's next, he had so many questions but yet he wasn't sure how they were going to proceed next. He could plainly see what the plan of action should be but he always knew that no plan ever survived first contact. His mind was a battlefield, he had survived countless moments of chaos and still came out the other side intact. He often thought whether that was due to the natural ability to land on his feet when falling or his training held him in good stead. Regardless of the outcome, all he knew was a life of violence in some form or another. As a child introduced to a life that would lead to the destruction of his mind. He had ended other people's lives and what for he had asked himself many times. He wasn't sure if it was for money or whether because that's the way he was trained. One thing for sure he knew and that he was good at what he done. He had stood silent and gave that nod whenever his father had given him new orders, decided by a group of shadowy men lead by greed. He often asked himself "Was it worth it?" That was something entirely different. He had killed for his fathers greed and need for dominance, for that he had honed himself into an assassin but yet he knew that final strike of the blade against his father was done through love rather than hate. He done it for all the people his father had hurt and that was definitely driven by love of his sister. Emiko was everything to him, he had spent every moment trying to protect her against their fathers greed. Even when he thought that he had witnessed her death, he wouldn't believe it until he had seen her body. He had tried to make peace with his demons and all that which had blackened his soul by every death. Even in this moment, he thought maybe he could complete this in some way of redemption. By locating this hidden cave of Hanzō's then maybe, just maybe he could redeem some honour of giving back to the people a piece of their history that could inspire the next generation. And then within that moment he knew what he would do. He looked at Sakai and made his decision.

CHAPTER ELEVEN

"I'll be totally honest with you Sakai-san, at first I wasn't sure where this path would lead, especially as it had some connection to my deceased father. I was hesitant whether to get involved with it, especially as these last few years I have avoided anything to do with my former life. You know my background and what I'm capable of, so I'm not going to insult your intelligence by trying to pretend that I haven't got my doubts. If this is and potentially could lead to one of the biggest finds of its kind, it could open a lot of doors, good and bad. I have battled with my conscience long enough to understand that we can find ourselves in that cave that Joseph Campbell described in his quote 'The cave you fear to enter holds the treasure you seek' But it is a journey I need to take to allow myself a form of redemption. I can't change all that I've done but maybe I need to do this regardless of the consequences. My greatest fear of all of this is that the wrong people learn of our good intentions and turn it into their own necessary evil for their own greed and gratification. But as long as we stay as undercover as possible, never swaying off that path, then it will work, especially if our location is good. What say you?" Ronin asked as he looked at Sakai, it as if he wanted to make that confession to gain an understanding of Sakai's true intent.

"Yes you are most correct Bailey-san, we do need to keep this to ourselves. For it was to get into the wrong hands then we could create a chain of events that are out of our control and this piece of history could be lost forever. I think we should spend the next couple of days working on establishing what kit we need, for we would be better to travel light to not gain any unwanted attention. Let's keep it as simple as possible and even if we do know that no plan ever survives first contact, at least we know what our challenges are. For if Yamada-san does learn of this, he would send those that would not show any mercy, you know who I'm speaking of. I know that you have came across them before within your lifetime that much I know of you. For I'm not going to treat you like a fool Bailey-say, for when you first made contact, I did quite an extensive background check as you can understand as I need to know who I'm getting involved with. Especially as I've had dealings with people who's true intentions are quite false when it came to this place. So many people try to gain some of these pieces by false intent and yet I have learned to see through them, I have a pretty good understanding of people and judge of them.

For when I looked into yourself, I had to separate facts from false statements to truly understand or gain a true perspective of a person. Regardless of the fact, your father was a cruel man and you did indeed make a lot of people suffer for his greed. But I think we can safely say, that you demonstrated your own vulnerabilities and soul when you fought him. It takes quite a person to come back from that but I can say that I have quite a level of good intentions that you display all together. Now let's get this moving forward, how about we meet again in 3 days to put our plans into action. It seems to be quite a good weather window for the next couple of weeks in the Iga region, so that will help us out. Let's get this done heh Bailey-san?" Sakai replied.

Ronin nodded and prepared to rise when a thought came to him. "Sakai-san, I only have one thing left to say until we meet again, it has taken a lot to get to this place today, to meet with you and for us to get this done, but believe me, this journey is much more to me than discovering the truth of Hanzō. It's about finding that measure of peace that I've been searching for a long time. Yes, it's important that we do this properly but also I'm able to rest a piece of my soul that's I've never been able to since that night. It's my time to give something back. That's why I will do everything to keep this as quiet as possible, it's simple to me. We turn up on location and get it done. In and out as quiet as possible, we use the cover plan as photographers, just makes it easier considering the beautiful area that we're heading into. Right, I'll get everything sorted my side and we'll meet up on location and move forward with it all, agreed Sakai-san?" Ronin asked. Sakai took one look at Ronin and smiled "Yes Bailey-san, agreed!"

Both men stood up and headed back to the entrance of the museum. Whatever was going to transpire in the next week will be what it is. Ronin had nothing more to consider in his plans. He had gone over every justification of his reasons and plans to get this completed as quietly and drama free as possible. The last thing he wanted was to be at odds with Yamada's men. He knew the lengths of brutality they could demonstrate and to him this was finding that small measure of peace in a worthy way. But he knew it is what it is and that's all it ever will be, the universe decides fate not you.

CHAPTER TWELVE

The kit lay out in front of him, he decided he would travel as light as possible but that didn't mean he wouldn't take his 'personal protection' it was ingrained in him, part of his DNA. His eyes wandered over the kit, it looked enough, the good part about his trade was that he didn't have to carry overly bulky kit. Yes, they would take a couple of firearms, but that is only needed is necessary and Ronin didn't fall back on a plan that was noisy. He knew if anything did happen, then it would be finished as quietly and quickly as it had started. He wasn't the kind of person that dealt in the ego game, making your presence loud and proud. That wasn't the way he worked. He preferred to get in, get the job done and get out without being noticed. It has not failed him yet that approach before.

He knew that he would need to prepare himself mentally a lot more than physically. Iga province was built up of mountainous, forested sections. It was easily travelled through for himself, but he knew Sakai may struggle with some parts, but nothing that couldn't be overcome. He had done his research on Iga, although he had learnt quite a bit over his life about it, especially in his teachings from his Sensei.

He knew that Iga province was a province of Japan, located in what is today part of western Mie Prefecture. Iga is classified as one of the provinces of Tōkaidō.

During the early Muronachi period, Iga became effectively independent from its nominal feudal rulers and established a form of republic. During this period, Iga came to be known as a center for Ninjutsu, claiming to be the birthplace of the Ninja clans.

In 1581, two years after a failed invasion led by his son, the warlord Oda Nobununga launched a massive invasion of Iga, attacking from six directions with a force of 40,000 to 60,000 men which effectively destroyed the political power of the ninja.

With the establishment of the Tokugawa shogunate, Iga was briefly ruled between 1600–1608 under the control of Iga-Ueno Domain, a 200,000-koku Han during the rule of Tsutsui Sadatsugu a former retainer of Toyotomi Hideyoshi. However, the Tsutsui clan was dispossessed in 1608, and the territory of the domain was given to Tōdō Takatora, the Daimyō of Tsu Domain. It remained a part of Tsu Domain until the Meiji Restoration.

As Ronin had been taught, within the Edo period, there were several well known people from Iga including Hattori Hanzō and also the famous Haiku poet Matsuo Bashō. Even Iga Ueno Castle was retained be Tsu Domain as a secondary administrative center for the western portion of the domains. Although, after the abolition of the Han system in July 1871, Tsu Domain became Tsu Prefecture, which then later became part of Mie Prefecture.

The problem with history as Ronin had found was that it moved so quickly and there was a lot that had happened within a relatively short period. He had always been fascinated with history, especially Japanese. Even as a child, he spent hours looking through detailed books covering images of Samurai and Ninja in his fathers study. It was the one place he found some peace and especially as not many people entered it, it had become a place that he could disappear to for hours. Even in his practical teachings, he could remember spending hours almost in playtime, climbing trees, crawling in silence up to a flag trying to capture it. As Ronin, knelt in front of his kit, be began to reminisce on his childhood. It was a place he remembers with some fondness but also a great deal of sadness. It was only in periods of meditation that his father had seen a use for him, especially after seeing his natural abilities within martial arts classes as a small child. Tanaka recognised great skill in Ronin, almost at a unnatural level even as a child compared to even some of his peers. Tanaka had manipulated that and turned what Ronin at the time was just playtime, into possibly one of the most effective assassins amongst the families. It was well known that the families employed assassins into their service to either silence a business partner or to simply prove that they couldn't easily be manipulated. But as Tanaka had proven, they were as he sent Ronin to 'remove' the threat to him and his business. He was a ruthless man and wouldn't stop until he had consumed as much as he could.

Throughout his childhood, Ronin used to see these games as fun time, just harmless games that any child would enjoy. He remembers as a child picking up the metallic objects laid out in front of him, he had already been warned of the sharp edges. All these different shapes and weights, Ronin wasn't sure what they were but he knew he liked them, especially the blades, whether it was the small thin blades or the star shaped ones. He found they fitted nicely within his hands, it was if they were meant to. He had even asked his Sensei whether these had all been made for him, his Sensei chuckled and replied "Bailey-Chan, this set has been in the family for a very long time, going back as far as the days of the samurai. But I'm sure the person who created them knew they would used by a great master one day, he just didn't know that it would be you"

It was through these periods of meditation that

Ronin realised how much of his childhood had been stained by the shadows of someone else's greed. Not as though he could do anything about that now. He had learned to live in the moment as he knew that there wasn't anything that he could have done to change what was before. He would often reply to his own questions with "What can you do?" He knew the answer was always going to be "Nothing" but it is what it is. With that he got to work with cleaning and packing the tools of his trade.

CHAPTER THIRTEEN

The screen lit up and he raised the phone up higher to see what was written, just a couple of lines but enough that it was time to go. He memorised the context and selected the option to delete it from the phone. It was something he had done multiple times and he often was relieved that it was just another disposable burner phone. But the last couple of words were always the last thing he burnt onto his memory 'Eliminate them' With that he put the phone down and swung his legs onto the floor, there was a chill in the air but that's not to be expected as he was surprised that he would be able to stand up straight after last nights storm. He lifted his body upright and stepped forward until he reached the door. He pulled down on the metal handle and opened the heavy door. He lifted his foot to step over the rim of the doorway. He steadied himself as he walked down the corridor until he came to the end. With a twist, he spun the watertight door and allowed the cool sea breeze to engulf him as he opened the door and stepped into what seemed like a shaken snow globe. But this time it was with droplets of water that were thrown over the railings. As he stepped forward he scanned across the vast ocean. It seemed like Poseidon himself had lifted the ocean from the seabed and thrown it upwards towards the midnight sun, leaving it to swirl and ripple on the surface. He steadied himself against the railings and took a massive gulp of sea air, he could taste the salt that lingered in his nostrils far longer than he ever imagined. It was time for him to work and that was all it was to him. Nothing personal, just work. Some people work at saving lives and others like him prostituted themselves for a fancy sum of money. He sold part of his body and soul every time he eliminated a target. But this time it was different, much different. As soon as he saw the name, he wasn't surprised as he knew he would show up sometime.

A thousand thoughts swirled around his mind after reading the target package. It often surprised him that the worst of jobs were passed onto him. He scanned the images and didn't need to read the text, he knew it better than the person who wrote it. But of course he would, he asked himself "How many times in your life do you get the chance to eliminate the person who assassinated your father, when they themselves were not even true blood of the family, just some imposter but forced to accept he was his brother" With one last breath, he turned around, still holding onto the railings and stepped forward. His jet black hair swept across his face, which he pushed away before making his way back inside the ship and prepare himself to visit death to ask for strength to do what must be done.

The light flooded in and engulfed the shape upon the futon on the floor. It twisted and moved until the sheet was thrown across and their legs were swung around until they reached the tatami next to the edge of the futon. The light of the early morning rays enlightened the picturesque scenery displayed across their wide muscular back. It was like a distressed canvas filled with lines and scars, light and dark shades splashed across a sea of different colours. Splattered and distorted in places, pure and sculptured in others. All that lay across their back told many a story, a life spun in ink. Mixed amongst the scars, some puckered, some smooth, others rough and ragged, earned over a lifetime of brutality. The dragon that wrapped around their torso was delicately infused with the delicate shapes and swift strokes, the boldest of colours, greens and blacks, trickled into place with a steady hand. Around the edges lay the sea that was bold and perfectly aligned as a background to the various designs, licking at their curvature with waves of white and shimmering blues. The body was positioned part on and part off the futon, ready to rise when a light shone next to their right hand. The phone came alive and displayed a text, bold and large across the screen. He had tweaked some settings to allow the full message to display without having to open the phone's Lock Screen. The message was clear enough, but confusing at the same time "The enemy of your enemy is 'not' your friend" he knew the saying well but without some kind of context he wouldn't make sense of it, especially with that added 'not' in there. He wasn't sure what to make of it, but then a thought occurred to him. He wasn't entirely sure if that meant that the one person who he thought all this time was an actual enemy was their friend, but thinking about it again he was almost certain that he was right, that was until his phone pinged again and a new message displayed above it 'Protect them at all costs, beware of the false sibling destined to gain a false crown' He was even more confused, but he didn't question the legitimacy of the message, especially for who it came from. He knew he would have to move quickly, even though he had been fully prepared for the week since the first message. He must do what he must and putting himself in harms way once more was nothing out of the ordinary. But this time it was different, especially after what had transpired in the last couple of years. As he stood, watching a fight unfold in front of his eyes, he saw the person who would change everything. But he certainly questioned the meaning of the text. If he was supposed to be his friend, then why was he told that he was his enemy but the one person that he was supposed to trust? But if he was meant to trust the source, then surely it will all be revealed he thought to himself. It didn't make any sense, especially as when he read it back again. So if Ronin was supposed to be the enemy, then that added 'not' must mean that in fact it was Tanaka was the enemy and not Ronin, this was getting crazy. But he trusted the source of the message, so he decided that he would go ahead with it. All these years had gone and yet Ronin was the enemy in many people's eyes. But as he stood there that night, he saw something in Ronin, it was if he was holding back, not wanting to fight back, there was humility in his stance and his manner. He decided to go ahead with his gut feeling and get the job done. But also he had noticed the package destination, labelled by three letters 'JPN' He stopped for one moment and thought to himself "Out of all the places on Earth, why Japan?" Either ways, that's the destination and he would find out more when he read the rest of the intel package. It was time to grab his stuff and get a move on if he was to catch the next flight out. As he grabbed his grab bag from the bottom of the wardrobe from concealed section, he didn't need to check as that was always done every few days depending on the possibilities of where is next assignment was. It was time to get a better understanding of what the hell was going on. He picked up his baseball cap and shades as he made his way to the door, time to earn his pay.

The air was filled with the sound of life but not

human, wind, birds and the sound of cicadas was like an explosion of noise in the morning breeze. But nothing would penetrate the internal meditations of the steel mind that was positioned against the breeze. The nostrils flared softly as the inhale created an airflow through the slightly parted lips. It was if a statue was placed in this idyllic garden. One that was wild and free of the burdens of the world in which it sat in. You would think it was a statue if it wasn't for the slow and soft inhale of air through the flared nostrils as well as the rise of the chest until it reached its pinnacle of expansion. Zoned out in this green and lush wonderland, the figure was in their element. A place they had spent many years exploring on daily basis as a child. Climbing trees, learning to navigate without even the bugs realising they were even there. Those were the days, the ones where everything was easy to understand. To them, it was a game. To focus and look back in reflection allowed them to gain a perspective of innocence placed upon them. On the wind, they would hear their name whispered, but then it all changed. He was no longer in this woodland but somewhere else, sitting on a mat surrounded by people, but they were unknown to them. They couldn't understand who they were, all they knew was the last words that was said before the stepped backwards towards the doorway. "Ronin, we've got to go, you may not see us again but we love you, just remember you're different from the rest. You're not like them, remember young shinobi, your day will come" and then nothing, they were gone, like smoke on the wind. Like a rush of light and sound, a cosmic explosion and he opened his eyes, fully focused. Ronin exhaled and scanned his surroundings, it was time to get this done.

CHAPTER FOURTEEN

He looked ahead and realised that what he was witnessing was an actual mountain and not just another hill. He had spent the last few hours preparing for the next couple of days. His discussions with Sakai had made him realise that this was bigger than he had ever imagined. What they were potentially going to do could change many perspectives of how people thought about Hanzō and not yet from an actual historical one. To many as Ronin had discovered and that which is quite common is that most people will except the narrative given to them that it flows in an A,B,C movement and that for example when Hanzō died, his body laid to rest Hanzō's in the Sainen-ji temple cemetery in Yotsuya, Tokyo with his favorite spear 'Yari' and his ceremonial battle helmet. The spear itself was originally 14 feet long and given to him by Ieyasu, it was donated to the temple by Hanzō as a votive offering, but was damaged during the bombing of Tokyo in 1945.

A lot is known historically about Hanzō. He was

known to be an expert tactician and a master of spear fighting. Historical sources say he lived the last several years of his life as a monk under the name of 'Sainen' and built the temple Sainen-ji to commemorate Tokugawa Ieyasu's elder son, Nobuyasu. When Nobuyasu was accused of treason and conspiracy by Oda Nobunaga, he was ordered to commit seppuku by his father, Ieyasu. Hanzō was called in to act as the official second to end Nobuyasu's suffering, but he refused to take the sword on the blood of his own lord. Ieyasu valued his loyalty after hearing of Hanzō's ordeal and said, "Even a demon can shed tears." Tales of his exploits were passed down and often attributed various supernatural abilities, such as teleportation, psychokinesis, and precognition, and these attributions contribute to his continued prominence in popular culture. At the time of his death, aged 55. There were a couple of versions of how he had died, was it natural causes or was there some foul play by being assassinated? Either way, Hanzō was a legendary character and so many people wanted to know what happened to his sword or even swords. Yes, his spear laid within the temple but even that had been damaged in the bombing of Tokyo in 1945, it was apparently originally 14 feet long which is quite some size considering that Japanese men are not as tall as Western men. That's longer than the length of two average sized men if they laid down head to toe and toe to head. Ronin tried to imagine what it was like to carry that into battle and the physical fatigue it would cause, not taking into consideration the weight of armour worn etc. But that's the problem with history, it is just a perspective given, it's not completely accurate.

Ronin had spent enough time preparing this day, at one stage he wasn't sure what he might discover. He wasn't even sure if he was possibly believing just rumours and not actual facts especially as he possibly held the key to a piece of Hanzō's past that was in contention. He wasn't sure what he would find but he also knew that himself and Sakai were the only ones after this prize. They had done everything they could do to cover their tracks, but as he knew all too well that no matter how well you think you've covered them, then there's always something left behind. They had double encrypted communications and used VPN's to change their locations several times. But no matter how good a plan could be checked, checked again and rechecked, then no plan ever survived first contact. This part of Iga was fairly remote and they had managed to travel in without too many people seeing them but Ronin also knew considering its history, these hills has eyes and ears everywhere, it had been a flurry of spying activities in its era. They had even approached it separately from two directions and even decided to stop some distance away from it and walk in. Everything they had done was to reduce any possibilities of their intentions. Ronin knew that Yamada was a formidable enemy, absolutely ruthless and would do whatever it took to claim the prize. That even included utilising one of his favourite assets only known as 'Higanbana' there was a lot of rumours associated with this person, even down to their name, Higanbana or otherwise known as Red Spider Lilies. It is a form of a bright summer flower that are native throughout Asia. But in any name, there are several meanings. They are associated with death and legend has it that these flowers grow wherever people part ways for good. In old Buddhist writings, the red spider lily is said to guide the dead through samsara, the cycle of rebirth.

However, Higanbana is just one of its names, one of them is the 'Flower of Death' It is poisonous to rodents and other wild animals, they were often planted in and around graveyards during Japan's pre-cremation days to stop the dead being eaten. Its bright colours are said to guide souls into the afterlife, this presumably explains its use at funerals. So if their nickname or identity is simply known as the 'Flower of Death' in the more common tongue then that says it all about them, Ronin had decided. He would need to be on full alert, not just for himself but also Sakai, for he knew what someone like Higanbana was capable of. He knew that because he recognised that in himself. Ronin never truly ever acknowledged of what he truly was and his true self, it was as if he went along with the motions, just accepting it. He had accepted it that he had never truly confronted his past, neither his present, only what was to come as he found that he had accepted his fate in the world, taking one more step towards his own destruction. Some people he found would never look inwards as they feared what they saw, Ronin never feared that because he knew what lay in there and even the brightest candle couldn't have lit that soul, even if he still had one. He never saw it as a form of self destructive behaviour but simply that he had accepted death a long time ago and relied on his skills with the blades and fists to outwit the cloaked master of his fate.

He had often questioned his own reasons for this journey. Maybe it was to delve a little deeper into himself. Possibly find a piece of redemption, knowing that he had done some good in this world before his time was called. To him, that was all it was. It was an hourglass of our calling, waiting for the last grain to fall.

CHAPTER FIFTEEN

The forest path wound round like a snake, through the undergrowth and soft beneath the feet. Ronin had decided that he would make his way in from a Easterly direction ad then meet up with Sakai on the southern point of the mountain. He had cut back a few times to through off anyone that would be following him. Even though he knew it would take him slightly longer, it was worth it. He didn't want anyone, especially Higanbana following his trail. He had often wondered if Yamada truly knew what was about to be attempted or was it another rouse or bait. He was not doubting Yamada's reach and influence but he had done everything he could to prevent any information from being leaked. He knew he was on Yamada's watchlist, especially after that last job. It seemed like Yamada had decided that because he was tasked to carry out the job and yet someone else had completed it, then he was the one responsible for its failure. Ronin had never truly understood that part and how he was responsible for information being leaked to another organisation. All that had happened was none of Ronin's creation, that was out of his control. And for anyone on Yamada's watch list, there was only one solution for disobedience and that was Higanbana. Ronin had heard rumours of what happened to those that had met them because there was several other rumours that Higanbana was never truly identified as a man or woman. All he knew was that he wanted to avoid them at all costs or that could lead to a fight that neither of them might not return from.

High above the ridge they watched, their eyes never wavered or deviated from the moving shape down below. They knew that he would have doubled back and made it as possible to be tracked but nothing would outsmart the one who was watching know. They knew exactly the way they operated and it was almost standard behaviour what they were watching now. But what they were wondering was the direction in which they were heading in. Even with the limited intel they had with the target package delivered via PDF only 12 hours ago. Half the time, they wondered how the intel was gathered so quickly, they knew Ronin was a master of his craft and yet he wouldn't have let anything leak or past the wrong person. They had stood by and watched Ronin in action many times and yet there was a slight fascination in how he was so surgical in his movements. The flow was perfect and dynamic. Some things still impressed the hell of them, more in absolute fascination how anyone can be that good. All that they thought they knew was just an illusion to what actually was. They had thought quite the opposite, all these years had gone by and yet they had believed that what they thought was the actual enemy may not be that at all. So confusing, considering the impression that had been sowed all this time. They had questioned many things in their time but this was definitely something that didn't make sense, especially after the last message and why send a target package? That's only for targets to be elongated and not protected. That must mean that someone else had a copy and they were the ones who were going to carry out that part. As they sat there watching the small shape slip and move in between the undergrowth beneath it all began to make sense now. If Ronin is not the enemy then there was someone else sent to eliminate them, but for what reason? There was quite possibly one person it could be, and was that what the puzzle meant? So many questions, but I guess all would be revealed soon enough.

They air was quite humid as Ronin made his way forward after cutting back and changing his path to throw off any chances to be followed. That was the last thing that they wanted, especially if Higanbana was knowledgeable about all of this in any way. He didn't trust many and if any information had been leaked then it hadn't come from Sakai, he knew that much as he was focused on potentially finding Hanzō's lost cave and sword. It wasn't a smart move at all, so Ronin had thought of many reasons of why Sakai would betray him but found none. Suddenly he stopped, he thought he saw something moving. He wondered if his eyesight was betraying him but there again he saw something. He stayed in a kneeling position as still as possible. He questioned whether it was his mind playing tricks, he scanned the ground in front of him and there again he saw what he thought was a child, dressed in black. It really was, a child no more than ten years old moving swiftly through the undergrowth in front of no more than 50 metres of him. He thought to himself "Why would a child be out here in the middle of nowhere?" He stayed in the kneeling position and just watched as he silently and swiftly moved through the undergrowth, only the air passing between them, it was if he was floating across the ground yet his feet were definitely touching the ground. Ronin gazed for a moment or two and suddenly it all clicked. What he was witnessing in front of him was a vision of himself as a ten year old child. The memories came flooding back, he was remembering now. It was at a time when he was learning how to move through undergrowth silently. Those lessons were ingrained within his mind. His Sensei waiting patiently on the other side of the forest after getting him to manoeuvre through this tough terrain allowing his ears and senses guide him through it as fast as possible. Originally, he was going to be blindfolded and sent through a set of obstacles but that was for the next level of his training. Firstly, he would have to learn how to move swiftly without a sound. He would have to trust his senses and gain an understanding of his footwork but Ronin had been doing smaller tasks for many years at this point. The thoughts and memories came flooding back, "Is this what he was experiencing now?" Ronin thought to himself as he watched the ten year old him stop in front and crouched down. Ronin thought maybe all these thoughts and emotions had come back as it was a particular important part of his life he had made him who he was today. He had spent a long time in these hills and forests learning so many different lessons and yet he had forgotten so much. He couldn't understand why they were coming back now. He had thought maybe it was due to getting closer to the potential location of Dragon Mountain and Hanzō's lost crypt. Ronin had thought to himself whether they would actually find it or it was just another lost journey.

Across the other side, about a kilometre from Ronin's location stood Sakai. He had made his way in from a different direction than Ronin, he had understood the need for silence on this especially if Higanbana had been sent to investigate the area. He had known about him for quite a few years. He hadn't met him and yet he had heard so much about him, especially his skills and rumours of his skill with a blade. Some had said that he could drop a man quicker with a blade than any gun. Sakai had done everything to keep their movements as secure as possible, all information was encrypted multiple times across various accounts. He had not stored any information on the Tsuba that Ronin had brought to him. He didn't want anyone to know about it. What did worry him though was the other rumours that he hadn't disclosed to Ronin and that was about Ronin's other family, his true family. Sakai had known his mother and father and what had happened to them. He wouldn't have wished that upon anyone. All Ronin had been left to know was that Tanaka was his father, who had become dangerous within the community. Especially when it came to riches. Tanaka had become obsessed with gaining more riches than any other family. He had cheated, stole and even murdered to gain more than anyone else. Sakai was standing watching the ground in front of him, waiting for Ronin to arrive. He did wonder whether he should keep any information about Ronin's family to himself as it wouldn't do any good. He knew that Ronin would at one point question his origins especially with his name as it wasn't exactly a Japanese name, yes Ronin is a masterless, wanderer and nomad. That Sakai knew all too well. He had heard the term given to many of the old samurai that had no master. But what intrigued him was why that title had been given to Ronin. Was it related to the rumours that he had heard a good few years ago he wondered "Only time will tell?" He thought to himself. He lifted his eyes and saw something move about 20 metres in front of him. He had wondered whether that was just a figment of his imagination when a voice spoke loud and clear behind him "Your thoughts are loud on the wind Sakai-san" came the voice. Sakai spun around to be greeted by Ronin.

"Your skills are more impressive than I had ever realised Bailey-san. One moment I thought I had seen something and then the next, you appeared behind me" Sakai said with an edge of fear in his voice. He knew that Ronin had an impressive set of skills but until had never witnessed them. Ronin looked at Sakai and simply said "We do what we must Sakai-san, to blend into the world around us is quite a skill even in the best of environments" Sakai took a moment to gather his thoughts, "Yes, that's very true Bailey-san, now to the task in hand. As we've previously discussed, this does seem to be the entrance for dragon mountain. Do you know if there was any sign of anyone within the area who could give away our position?" Sakai said. Ronin had thought he had seen something upon a ridge line high above. Even if there had of been, there wasn't much he could have done from that distance. All he could do was to do what he did best and that was to get in and get the job done, simple as that. He pulled out the plastic covered map that had been blown up to concentrate on the area in which they were in. They had opted to not bring in any phones etc to minimise their digital signal, some tasks require old school tactics. He looked at the map for another moment before turning it around and using a toothpick pointed towards a section. "So here you can clearly see our location Sakai-san, it's between these two hills. Also, what we can see ahead is a path that winds down through this ridge, from the air it must look like a mouth in which we're entering, at least it gives us some hope that we're actually in the right location. If we follow this path, it should lead us to a possible entrance. Only problem is that we're not able to switch back and lose any potential trackers following. I've been spending as much time trying to throw anyone off our tracks but if Higanbana is aware of our movements, which I can only hope that they are not as we both know where that would lead. Also, there is also the possibilities of Yamada sending in a small army. So we've got to move swiftly and as silently as possible from now on, are you good with that?" Ronin said, looking straight into Sakai's eyes, searching for any doubts but he saw none. Yes there was that natural fear that was understandable but no doubts. Sakai shook his head and simply replied "Yes Bailey-san, let's go" They both turned and started off in the direction off the path in front of them.

High above on another ridge line, watching the small figures trek off, a smile appeared upon their face, almost a grin, knowing that they had fallen into their own trap. No way out except for the awaiting contingency of men waiting for them to collect the prize. Knowing they didn't need to get their hands dirty for this one pleased them. Yes, Ronin was a possible problem, but they knew him quite well and was assured by their men's skills, especially as they had trained them as good as they had trained with Ronin, even now they didn't approve of that name. Why he couldn't have used his true name but yet the name they had grown up calling him was quite suitable, especially as he was masterless, he was a nomad and wanderer. The English family that had adopted him after his true family were silenced had named him after their own but that was only for a few years until Tanaka-san had tracked him down and took him on as his own, but in the agreement, he had agreed to keep Ronin's name as it was. Well, the family were especially well off now after the deal. It seemed like Tanaka-san could buy whatever he wanted. With that fading thought, they looked down upon their watch and typed two words 'Dragons Den' before sending it. Now it was time to sit and wait, it was a waste of time sending in men to get the prize, plus Ronin's element was within the shadows, "Let him come out to play within the light and see what comes next" they thought to themselves.

CHAPTER SIXTEEN

The path ahead was narrow and sloping, it was not ideal terrain to counteract an ambush but Ronin had to deal with whatever came his way. He had dealt with worse but he was sure that he had put enough countermeasures in place even though as Murphy's Law states 'If anything can go wrong, it will' and that's something that Ronin was good at. He knew that if it's going to go wrong then he would find a way to win, simple as that. All he wanted to do was to get to that cave and see for himself if the rumours about Hanzō were true. If they were then that would change everything. He had spent countless hours putting every plan into place, even the motion detectors that he had placed in the entrance to pick up on any movement in the direct arc of the area in front of the path, even Sakai didn't realise that he had done that, he had distracted him long enough to place the devices. It wasn't as though he didn't trust him, but it was one less thing to worry about. If Yamada had deployed Higanbana on this task which was highly likely, then Ronin wanted to be fully prepared. He had been dubious about one potential flaw in the plan. Although he had secured all comms between him and Sakai, the only place he had no control over was the museum, he had heard of bugs being placed within it to pick up on any intel. Especially as there were rumours of Yamada employing others to gather intel with concealed equipment. He had a far reach and then he used Higanbana to carry out his dirty work. Ronin had heard of all the various theories that Yamada wanted to own the largest collection of original and uniques swords as well as armour and what better place to gain that intel than a museum that housed swords and armour. Ronin had done everything he could to have covered his tracks but there was only so much he could do. If Yamada knew that they were out here, then all he could do was to prepare for the worst, he then thought of something that swirled around his mind

'Life without structure is called chaos, but chaos with structure is called a plan. Prepare for the worst so you can succeed with the best' That was something he lived by. He always planned to the last detail but as he knew all too well and that was that 'No plan ever survives first contact' another worthy quote. Even if it did go to worst case scenario, then he had thought of a few options that he could fall on, but that wasn't something he wanted to rely on. He had prepared for as many eventualities as possible but he knew that even the best plans don't execute the first time.

As they walked along the path, Ronin knew that whatever happened next would be the biggest event in his life and although he wasn't sure what was next to come, he was ready. Sakai had been pretty quiet for the last few minutes and turned to Ronin to ask a thought that was swirling in his mind. "So what do you think we'll find Bailey-san? Do you think we'll discover the lost blade of Hanzō or do you think it is truly a myth?" He asked Ronin as they walked at a quick pace. Ronin thought about the question for a moment or two before answering. "To be honest with you Sakai-san, I'm not entirely sure what's next, if we have the Tsuba and it really is Hanzō's then there may be some truth to it. As for a lost cave that's filled with Hanzō's true resting place then that could change everything. If Yamada truly believes that it does exist then he'll do whatever it takes to get to it. I've heard all the rumours about Higanbana myself but until now, that's all they've been. But I do know this, I've been feeling as if we are being followed since we set off. Even though we've been clever enough to avoid detection up to this point, then if Yamada is sitting back and waiting for us to claim the prize only to take it from us when we emerge then we are prepared" Ronin said as he placed his hand upon his pack slung across his back which contained his blade. He had come prepared and even though you couldn't see them, he had prepped himself with a selection of his blades including his trusty hidden wrist blades that were his best weapon as they didn't see them until it was too late. "Let's get down this path and see if there really is a portal into Hanzō's hidden world. It shouldn't be too far and then we shall know, I'm not keen on the location as this path is fairly secluded but it's slope to the right of us has its gaps in the trees that can allow an ambush to be established. If I'm correct in the details, we should be nearly there Sakai-san" Ronin explained as they got closer to the overhang and the path dipped down towards a potential entrance. "Yes, you are right Bailey-san, we've done everything we can and let's hope it's been enough but not everything goes to plan first time does it? I'm guessing that this path does lead us to an entrance" Replied Sakai as they started a descent underneath the overhang. Ahead they could see a rock face which had a doorway shape carved out of it. As they got nearer, they could see an area to the left of it that looked like a fist size indent. They stopped in front of it and looked at each other. Sakai nodded to Ronin as Ronin slipped his right hand into a haversack next to his waist. He pulled out the wrapped Tsuba and started to pull back on the cloth covering it. He wasn't sure but it felt as though there was some kind of vibration through it, as if was connected to its home. He lifted it up next to the gap and held it between his fingers, positioning it and aligning it in the gap. He pushed it in and then they both heard a click and waited. Nothing happened at first and then Ronin lifted his left hand and placed it upon the doorway, he looked at Sakai and gave a grin as he pushed forward. The doorway cracked open with a gentle push "Whatever lies ahead Sakai-san will determine our fates, no path ever walked is the easiest when the darkness is cloaked around us but with the right light, it eases the footsteps we place upon its enlightened path" Ronin said as he pushed harder and removed the Tsuba from the gap. "Are you ready Sakai-san?" Ronin asked, "More than ready Bailey-san" replied Sakai as he watched Ronin step over the threshold into the mouth of the deep.

As they stepped into the depths of the darkness, Ronin brushed Sakai's arm "I'll lead Sakai-san, I'm used to these environments and if I'm right in believing that there could potentially be some possible booby traps ahead, I would rather face the consequences than yourself" Ronin said as he moved forward. He stopped for a moment and slid his hand into a small pouch on his side where he pulled out a head torch "Better to come prepared, or should I say that it is definitely better to bring something we may not need rather and not use it than something we need and not have eh Sakai-san"explained Ronin looking at Sakai. "Yes, you are right Bailey-san. I used to be pretty good at navigating throughout the darkness but that was many years ago and age has crept up on me now" Sakai replied. They both slid the torches over their heads and activated them. A bright beam shone ahead of them guiding the path ahead. Ronin excelled in environments like this, even though he knew he had prepared with the right kit, even he didn't know what lay ahead of him. He would take it slow as anything could be in their way.

As they moved slowly along the narrow passage, their hands moving along the rough rock face, feeling the grooves and indentations within it to grip to if needed. Judy moving through the darkness brought back quite a few memories of his youth. He thought back to being taught the way of stealth and navigating through similar obstacles, using his senses and hands, slowly working his way through a dark cavern without the use of any optical aid. He had learned to zone in to the darkness, concentrating on his footing and guiding his hands across the rough rock faces and outcrops. Even in environments like this can induce claustrophobia, it can make you feel as though your going crazy with the thought of being trapped. But that was the first lesson he learned, it was all within his breathing and concentration. No amount of enclosed environments would defeat his mind and this was the first lesson of becoming one with his environment.

As they approached a bend in the tunnel, Ronin looked ahead and saw a gap that looked like it headed into a cavern of some kind. He indicated to Sakai what was ahead and pointed in that direction. Sakai nodded and followed Ronin, confident in knowing that he was leading them in the right direction. As they approached the gap, Ronin stopped and slid his hand into another pouch that was strapped to his side, he pulled out a cylindrical object and unscrewed the cap from the top of it, before pulling the tag which initiated a bright light which literally flared he turned his head away so his night vision wasn't affected. The flare lit the cavern ahead which was actually quite a size. He threw the flare ahead of him and watched as it bounced a couple of times before laying on the floor of the cavern, illuminating it in all its size. They both looked in amazement at a cavern which literally was the width and length of a large hall. Aligned on either sides were statues of samurai and a path that led up to some kind of doorway carved out of the rock. They were both silent, just standing looking around and scanning the immense cavern ahead of them.

Sakai was the first to speak after a few minutes, "Bailey-san, I cannot believe it. I had a feeling that there may be some truths in the rumours but this..... I never expected anything like this. Shall we proceed" he said as Ronin nodded. "Yes we shall Sakai-san, although we must be careful, there may be some kind of booby traps ahead of us as the path behind could easily have been easy fooling us to drop our guard. I fear that if Hanzō wanted others to discover this then he would have made it knowledgeable to everyone, we must tread with caution" he replied. Ronin dropped his foot down upon the first step that led down onto the cavern floor, he told Sakai to wait there in case it triggered any booby traps. As he moved his heel down upon the step and then gently allowing the ball of his foot to drop down so his weight was displaced more easily as he wasn't sure if there was any booby traps ahead that were activated by his body weight. Slowly repeating the action, he finally got to the bottom step and turned around to signal to Sakai to follow him. He watched as Sakai slowly made his way down until he was behind him.

"Sakai-san, I feel as though it may all change from here on. The pathway ahead looks easy enough to walk straight up to, but as you know with reading the same intel as myself, Hanzō was a master of his craft and Ninjutsu traps are quite technical at times. Sometimes weight activated and other times it could be a simple trip wire that is used. I think it would be best to try and trick the path ahead in case there is anything ahead" Ronin explained as he looked at Sakai. "I couldn't agree more Bailey-san, with limited intel on this cave, anything can happen. What do you have in mind?" Sakai replied as Ronin pulled out another flare and nodded for Sakai to turn his head. As he did so, another bright flare of light spewed out of the tube and Ronin carefully threw the flare towards the centre of the path and waited.

CHAPTER SEVENTEEN

J ust as they thought they may have been safe after a few seconds, they both heard a deep clunk which was never good and as they looked back, a solid slab of rock slid down over the entrance they had both entered. The small slit of light in the distance was extinguished and they were left enclosed in the darkness. Nothing was said for a for a few moments until Ronin spoke. "Sakai-san, do you remember reading the lettering on the bottom of the map?" He asked. He took a couple of seconds before Sakai replied, "Yes Bailey-san, I do. It was quite cryptic but makes sense now you ask. If I'm right, it stated 'A foot is only a foot but when placed lightly it covers a larger distance than many metres, quite confusing when thinking about it. But I take it that it speaks of the path ahead of us and that we must tread lightly. That was just one of the challenges I guess. As we progress, I feel that these challenges will become more difficult, what says you Bailey-san?"

Ronin scanned the area ahead of him, placing the beam on the cracks around the slabs, looking to see any potential traps or wires, without seeing any he looked at Sakai. "Yes Sakai-san, you are correct, we must be careful what lies ahead. At least we know something, and that is if Yamada has sent Higanbana to capture a potential prize then their entrance is sealed shut, even if they use any kind of explosives to breach the cavern, then it will only alert us or bring down the ceiling on themselves. Either ways, we're prepared for any eventualities" he said whilst patting a haversack secured to his waist. He said no more leaving Sakai pondering on what he was carrying as he turned to face the next part of their journey.

Ronin placed one foot down slowly, toes placed upon the slab before allowing his heel to make contact with the stone. As he looked ahead he noticed that the slabs were aligned in a form that worked their way towards the carved doorway. But what made him look closely was the way the some of the slabs were risen and others were slightly lower, he wasn't sure if that was a good sign. As he moved forward he kept looking at the slabs to notice if they moved beneath him when he stood on them. He turned back at looked at Sakai. "Sakai-san, I'll move ahead a few slabs, just in case they are booby trapped, if my weight doesn't activate them, then we should be good, but I have a feeling that it's going to get a lot more cryptic as we carry on" Ronin said as he turned back to carry on moving forward, just as Sakai was about to answer after he had placed his foot upon the slab in front of him, there was a clunk and that to him was never a good sign. Suddenly, there was a whoosh of air and in a split second reaction that Sakai couldn't understand how it was done Ronin had twisted his body to face him and grabbed him by the lapels of his jacket, pulling him down towards him as the air was split by a metal object being fired towards him. Everything had gone into slow motion and the look in Ronin's eyes was that this was going to get a lot worse as the silence in his mind dissolved although he had broken through the water into the cold air and sounds came rushing towards him with vengeance. "Run now, towards the door" Ronin shouted as they twisted their bodies to align themselves towards the doorway. Sakai knew it was now or never as time sped up to meet reality and they both set off towards the carved doorway whilst hell erupted behind them with several metal objects splitting the atmosphere around them and striking some of the statues that stood on their right. Ronin was impressed how fast a man of Sakai's age could move this quickly, but anyone would if their life was on the line.

They reached the carved rock face and placed their hands upon the cold hard surface, drawing in as much oxygen as their lungs would allow them to. After a few moments Ronin spoke "Well Sakai-san, I think we can be confident that this was never was going to be easy but also confirms that Hanzō is not the kind of person that would allow the wrong people into his domain. It seems that part of the puzzle I have begun to understand. It does seem that it would take the swiftest and boldest warrior to transverse these challenges. Only the cleverest of Shinobi could make their way through each challenge or trial as written on the map. If you remember rightly, there was a part that stated 'Dark as night, silent as the wind upon the storm and all those pass that walk into the dragons mouth' well I think we can safely say that this is indeed the dragons mouth and these trials tested the skills of the greatest shinobi. I know why those slabs were different levels to each other. It was to give off the illusion they were booby trapped at certain ones but in reality once we had crossed over the line on the first one and the slab had dropped to cover the doorway, it switched them, so what we thought was the safe path was indeed weight activated once I had stood upon them. And those shuriken's that were fired from the wall were designed to test your speed and agility. Right, let's get through this doorway and then worry about what's next, what say you Sakai-san?"

Sakai had caught his breath but had to wipe his forehead as the sweat had started to build upon it. He wasn't surprised after that. He still couldn't understand how Ronin had done what he he had seen. This made him think twice of who he was.

He had heard the rumours but brushed them off until now, he hadn't thought anyone could posses such skills but he wouldn't question any more at this time. He looked at Ronin and nodded. "Yes Bailey-san, let's get through into the next part and see what faces us, that is the best idea I've heard all day" he replied.

The rock face held another carved section which perfectly housed the Tsuba. A click and the rock door led through into what looked like a passage, but there was only so much seen through the beam of light emitted from the head torch. Even if Ronin had used his Night Vision Goggles, that would only work if there was any kind of light source but within these conditions, there wasn't any, it was pitch black. Ronin was wary of what was ahead of him and slowly moved ahead using his feet to sweep in front of him, he was wondering if there was any weight activated devices beneath him just waiting to be activated and the walls to crush them. But that was his mind spiralling out of control. He had to take a good few box breaths to control his anxiety. Four seconds in, two out and repeat. He turned back and looked at Sakai. Even though he wasn't showing it but he could see in his eyes that the same level of fear was flowing through him as he was experiencing but he knew he would have to bottle that and turn it into action.

As they reached the end of the passage, Ronin

could feel a slight cool flow of air upon him as he moved forward. They had reached what seemed like another cavern but not as large as the original one, a thought had gone through his mind. There was in fact a few that had flowed and swirled around it over the last couple of hours, he wasn't sure if there was any facts to them but maybe he should discuss them with Sakai as he wasn't even sure they even made any sense. As his hands felt along the rock, his fingers seemed to curl around a corner as his head torch illuminated the area ahead of him. Of what he could see in front of him it was indeed a smaller cavern but something was different from the last one. From the ceiling hung long poles either side of it. When he placed the beam more directly on them, he could see that they were one in front of the other, maybe ten or fifteen in total and they all were angled like a triangle shape. All he could presume was that they formed rafters but no joists to form a traditional roof. But there was something different about these as the ends glinted when the light hit them, all he could presume was that they formed blades so maybe he was right what he was thinking especially as just behind the last ones were solid objects on either side of the cavern. All his thoughts had tumbled into one and although one of his thoughts had gone back to a couple of books he had been reading through before he travelled across. One of them was 'Reflections on the Art of Living: A Joseph Campbell Companion' which consisted of material selected and edited by Diane K. Osbon. The following text appeared in a section titled 'In the Field'

'It is by going down into the abyss
that we recover the treasures of life.
Where you stumble,
there lies your treasure.
The very cave you are afraid to enter
turns out to be the source of
what you are looking for.
The damned thing in the cave
that was so dreaded
has become the center.
You find the jewel,
and it draws you off.
In loving the spiritual,
you cannot despise the earthly'

There was also 'The Hero's Journey' but the theme ran through it was very similar. As he himself stood within this cavern, he thought back to its context. In the ancient world, caves were crucial for many rites of passage. These tunnels were both passages to the underworld, as well as the earth's womb from which initiates were reborn and transformed into their true versions of themselves. In ancient rites, initiates departed the relative comfort and warmth of familiar worlds, entering this mysterious world shrouded by the unknown and also unseen challenges. Maybe this is what he was meant to be doing and why he was here, but what about the challenges? All his thoughts focused on one element, his childhood. Where most children would play football or soccer, with their friends building treehouses etc he had spent his in the surrounding areas playing games that tested his wits and agility, one of them was the log game. Logs would be swung one after another each other and he would have to avoid each one as they swung back and forth alternating in their motion. It was like a trial he was being tested for, all these little games testing his abilities, agility, speed and strength. He had once heard rumours of it being referred to as 'The trials of the Shinobi' where young Ninja's were tested before they could go out and test their skills for real. But also, when he thought twice about it, they had entered that cave or cavern which was larger, gone through a trial to enter a smaller one, unaware of what was next and what was at the end of? Maybe this was his rebirth, his redemption, whatever it was, it would surely change his perspective. There was only one way and that was forward.

Ronin stopped and turned to face Sakai, who was right behind him, a little worn out and weary looking. Ronin spoke first "I think this path is for me and only me at this point Sakai-san, I wasn't sure at first, but this journey so far has brought us to this place. We've entered the womb of the cave and now we're here, ready to move forward, are you ready for a rebirth because this is how it feels to me. The Ninja were well known for their spiritual practices and even some into the dark arts. This next stage won't be difficult and I'm sure that Hanzō wouldn't have wanted it to be, only the best of the best could survive this trial to enter the final cave. If anything, if Yamada knows anything about this cave which might have only found out some elements about it, then he would definitely be wiser for someone else to complete it and bring him back the reward. That would end up with us falling right into Higanbana's grasp and what a fight that would be. Yamada's greatest warrior, unknown identity for a reason. I'm not concerned about Yamada's foot soldiers, their nothing, just bait. But Higanbana is something different, weirdly so but I feel connected to them, whether they're male or female. But we shall see what happens, I'm prepared for whatever comes our way. What says you?"

Sakai looked a little taken back but ready to move forward "Yes Bailey-san, you're right. This is no easy task ahead and Yamada knows this, I'm not sure myself how he would even find out about our journey, all I can presume is that he would have bugged the museum and I would definitely be on his list for persons of interest with overseeing the museum with all its historical content. I have over the years been approached by several individuals that are more than likely connected to Yamada wanting to purchase several items that are within the museum but I've refused. The content of it isn't to boost someone's ego but it's a part of our history and that's to be valued. You on the other hand, I'm really starting to believe that this is personal to Yamada. Whatever reason he has against you I'm not sure, but I do know that once you're on his radar, he will hunt you down and extract whatever he's interested in. There has always been one part though that's intrigued me since we've connected though Bailey-san?" Sakai asked whilst looking directly at Ronin.

Ronin looked a little puzzled, but answered back a little hesitant "Yes Sakai-san, and what's that?"

CHAPTER EIGHTEEN

"Your name Bailey-san, I'm intrigued. You were born to English parents yet brought up the Japanese way. Bailey is a very English surname and Ronin is a Japanese term for a drifter or wanderer, a masterless Samurai. So why did you not take Tanaka as your surname? Surely as Tanaka-san adopted you and brought you up, he would have wanted you to carry his name?" Sakai asked.

Ronin did not miss a beat as he replied, he had this script deep within his mind for when the time was right. "Simply because that is what I am, I am a Gaijin, an outsider, an alien. To Tanaka, I am and always will be a foreigner, non Japanese. Tanaka wanted me for one reason and that was for what I could do for him. He used and manipulated me to build his wealth and power. I was simply a chess piece on which he could play me from a child. As for Ronin, I will always be masterless. I have no real family left except my sister Emiko and even though she's not my blood sister. She always will be that to me. I am what you call a commodity, an asset to carry out Tanaka's bidding. Even in my dreams, I still see their faces fading into the dark, my mothers hand reaching out as I try and grab hold. You may wonder why I'm being so free to share all this with you Sakai-san? I've held this within for more years than I care for. I've seen life and death and everything in between. I no longer want to see death or suffering and yet here I am walking amongst the world with blood on my hands. My soul is as blackened as they come, nothing left. I trust you Sakai-san as I sense no greed or malice within you. I knew that there are many that walk the path of searching for lost treasures and yet they do it for the glory and ego but not you, you truly want to unlock all these secrets and give it back to the people of Japan, for their pride and history, I commend you for that" Ronin said as his words drifted off as his eyes shifted away from Sakai.

Sakai was quiet for a few moments as he stood there contemplating his next word. He had never expected Ronin to be as deep as that, he knew most of his history from the research he had done but nothing compared to what he was hearing. It was though Ronin had accepted fate and embraced death, well beyond the level of comprehension that he had known himself. But would he probe any deeper in Ronin's past? He decided that he would leave it for now until Ronin was willing to talk again. He looked at him and simply said

"Thank you Bailey-san, that means a lot, so what's next? Do you think we will discover Hanzō's lost treasures and secrets once we get past this point?"

Ronin thought about that very question, and at the point of not being very sure he spoke "Sakai-san, I can only guess the answer is like ourselves, we can remember our youth like yesterday but it was a lifetime ago. If Hanzō really thought of laying his blade in front of us it was meant to happen but as we've seen so far, it wasn't meant to be taken so lightly. I hasten to guess that this journey we've taken so far is a test of ourselves. All we know from the map is this is a possible location but then again, we may have to travel to the very coastline of Japan and beyond before we discover his true intentions. We know he was supposed to have retired as a monk but that doesn't answer our question of where he lay. Graves are often silent platforms for the dead often speak. We get past this point and then what's next I ask you? Are we even meant to reach the next stage for I know that these tests would only apply to the greatest and swiftest of warriors or you're not worthy as indicated by that skeleton over" Ronin said as he pointed to a mound of white and dark shapes but when focused on was indeed a human skeleton.

They both stared at the skeleton laying there, there was a dark hole on the side of the skull that both of them didn't need to guess what it was. They turned and faced each other, both silent for a few moments until Ronin spoke "Well I think it's best to say that maybe I should go first Sakai-san, but if I don't make it, I want you to carry on, I will do everything I can to make it to the other side. I'm not afraid of death Sakai-san, in fact I embrace it. Once you accept it, it no longer has a hold on you" he said and turned to face what was head of him. Sakai wasn't even sure what to say after that so all he simply said "Of course Bailey-san, I understand. Have you ever faced anything like this before?" Ronin was fully focused on the task ahead of him, but he heard Sakai's question and it did make him think about it for a moment or two. "Many years ago as a child, but I think I can safely say that I've changed since then but I have a good understanding of what I'm facing if it is the same" He spent a few moments studying what was ahead of him and how the poles interacted. He faced Sakai and spoke in a low tone,

"I breathed the dark
Until the light radiated within
I can see the shadows
Of my soul dancing
In the light of the night"

As Ronin voice drifted off at the end of his Haiku, or Japanese death poem he turned to fully face the challenge ahead.

Many thoughts were flooding Ronin's mind in that particular moment. He knew what was ahead and what he faced. This particular trial was going to test him to his physical limits. He had heard many things about it. It was apparently, once the events had been set in motion and it began, your body and mind had to to work in unison to survive it. There were many that tried and failed. It was more a mental battle than anything. All his thoughts flowed back to his childhood in that time, memories of trying to achieve the almost impossible. Knowing what was ahead was ultimately daunting as much as it was thrilling. He knew in that moment, he would simply embrace death as once he had done that, it would not have a hold upon him. He was free of his physical mind and body, to enter a place of peace he had not known and upon that path he was prepared to step. This journey to him was everything that his life had led up to. He wasn't sure if he would find the redemption that he had searched for. For death had surrounded him like a cloak all his life. He couldn't even remember how it started but he damn sure knew how it ended. He started to conduct breathing exercises to ready his lungs to not worry about filling enough oxygen to get him through. Four seconds of deep breathing, hold and exhale for two and repeat. He continued until he had reached a point of clarity. The adrenaline flowed through him aggressively after that initial drip, drip, drip and the tap had been turned on fully. He was ready, it was time. He focused ahead and positioned his body, every muscle and sinew tightened and flexed like a bow ready to be drawn, the arrow notched and the bow aligned towards its target. Drawn back and with the grace of the gods met it's mark ahead. It was time. One last exhale......

Ronin's feet left it's loose grip upon the rocky ground and launched ahead, after the first contact with the smooth floor beneath which was loosely covered with a millennia of dust and particles, he heard an ominous thud. The adrenaline smashed through his body like a whitewater river against the rocks as he awaited for the first pillar to meet him. He could feel the vibration of it swinging towards him upon his left, hurtling, building up momentum as it travelled to impact his body and break it. Ronin's arms and lungs were working as fast as humanly possible as he made his way along the path. If his timings were correct he would have less than a second to avoid the first pillar at its peak and that time was nearly there. He resisted the urge to close his eyes and relying on his senses. He could sense the pillar hurtling towards him at an incredible speed. "One more step, that's all it would take, could he make it" he screamed through his mind as he reached the point of no return.

But it wasn't just one he faced, there were six. All meeting at that singular point of time to crush his body if he was a second late and what was worst was the fact that they were lined with sharp spikes, evidently displayed up the the skull, as what caused their death. Ronin felt as though time and space had collided in an incredible supernova. The vacuum that was almost caused with six pillars coming towards him to shift his body a little too much but he held true to his mark and pushed on. He was entirely focused upon end point like an arrow that had been released upon flight and ready to meet its maker. It was if time and space had ceased to be as his foot met the mark he had planned ahead of him. Ready or not.......

CHAPTER NINETEEN

As Ronin's foot met that mark he had predicted in front of him, there was a few events that rolled into one. A deep heavy clunk was heard that vibrated deep within the cavern. He knew he had set off a chain of events that he was ready to face. He switched off from the fact that the pillars to the left and right of him were ready to swing across and potentially try and go through him. But he had already disconnected from that thought as this is what fear does. It impacts your mind, allowing it to be overwhelmed by multiple thoughts at once until it becomes a cloud of confusion. But never had Ronin felt more clarity than now. His timings were accurate in his mind as he awaited the last chain reaction to happen, releasing the pillars to swing. His aim and focus was exactly ahead of him and he became more determined than ever to reach the other side. And then it happened. He felt a shift in the atmosphere around him, it was if though it was being pulled away from him but also against him, designed to either slow him down or knock him off his path. As he built momentum, he also picked up speed as he ran faster than he had ever done. He would need to reach past the point of breaking, his lungs began to burn as the oxygen he inhaled through his nostrils heated and flooded his bloodstream. Every step he took and felt his foot touch the rock beneath them was one step closer to the end goal.

And then it happened. This was it, getting closer as the pillars began their final descent towards him. The tips of the spikes built into them driving towards him. His timings would need to be perfect as they drove forward with incredible speed. Being hit by any of these pillars would be like being crushed by a speeding truck. Not only would it crush every bone in the impacted area, the spikes themselves would impale themselves in him and tear his flesh.

One more step to go, the vacuum caused by these stone pillars was intense, but yet again he held true as he reached that maximum impact area. Ronin was fully prepared to meet his maker as his right foot touched the rock beneath him and almost felt the rock touch his face as it swung past him, as one would go past the opposite pillar would also move past him creating a pathway ahead, almost like the roof of a temple. It was almost a moment that Ronin could not believe was happening, he had welcomed death and cheated it as he made his way through the path ahead which had opened up as the pillars reached either side of him, as they swung towards their impact area on opposite walls, Ronin expected the noise to be deafening as they struck them but nothing which was oddly weird. But then he realised that they must of been attached slightly off the wall at their maximum swinging angle.

Just as he reached the gap created by the last pillar, a cold chill flooded through him as he saw a gap between him and the rock wall ahead of him. It looked like some kind of dead mans ground. His lungs and legs screamed for him to slow down and stop whilst his mind screamed back to keep going. He knew this wasn't the end and there was more to come. He fully focused on the end as another shift in the atmosphere happened, at first it was very small, almost unrecognisable. And then he saw it, a small wire that glinted off the beam from his heard torch. This must be either a trip wire that released a onslaught of sharp blades that would strike him at furious speeds tearing through his body or another devious device sharp enough to slice through his ankles removing his feet from his legs. Either ways it wasn't going to happen as he learned slightly back and lifted his front foot off the rock floor whilst he used his body weight to push his back foot off the floor a fraction later. He launched himself forward and over the wire, now it was time to concentrate on his descent before he impacted the rock wall ahead. His front foot angled towards the floor to touch down upon the sole of it allowing him to to tuck his body into a forward roll as he reached forward with his left arm. But then it struck him. As he looked ahead he saw a difference in colour of the rock.

This was known as a 'Leap of Faith' a deep chasm between two rock formations. Even if Ronin had successfully navigated the spiked pillars and the wire, his last part was to leap over this chasm and allow his body to accept whether it was going to make it or not by how much momentum he had built upon his approach.

Ronin looked ahead at the exact point in which he wanted to land. He was fully focused, all thoughts were put to one side as he prepared himself mentally to literally take a leap of faith. He turned to Sakai and started to unclip his pack off his back when he spoke, "Sakai- san, could you look after this please, don't worry though I'll be back for it when I've done this" Ronin asked. He nodded and replied, "Of course Bailey-san" as he reached out to accept it, he knew what was in that pack and he knew that he would indeed be back for it. He stood back and watched.

Sakai stood silent as he observed Ronin in his body movements and language. He had every faith that he would make it, he wasn't sure what it was about him but he just knew that he wouldn't fail. He stood as silent as he had ever been as Ronin took a good few steps back and ground his feet into the rock beneath them, his arms were positioned beside him, slightly tense but relaxed at the same time. And then he saw it, the moment of energy being transferred through him as he leant forward before his body exploded in an incredible display of energy being released.

In that very moment, nothing existed within Ronin's mind except that one point on the other side. As he built up momentum, he switched off from everything external and allowed the adrenaline to flow through him as he powered ahead until he reached the edge of the chasm. His foot reached the point of the last place where it could physically grip the earth beneath him and launched into open space. Nothing beneath him, everything ahead of him. Time slowed down as he reached ahead, connecting to the physical space ahead of him. He leant forward as he aimed towards the rocky edge ahead and prayed.

CHAPTER TWENTY

His foot touched the rocky surface ahead and pushed down as he reached forward to throw himself into a forward roll. Transferring all his energy into a landing of some kind. As his arm folded at an angle to take the impact of the fall, his body followed the trajectory of his body and his legs finally landed with a thud upon the rocky floor. All time and space came rushing back as he exhaled a massive rush of oxygen and lay there with no thoughts except elation, he had made it. It took a few moments to realise that Sakai was shouting his name.

"Are you ok Bailey-san? Are you injured?" The voice came to him like he was exiting a dream. Ronin rolled over into his side and looked at Sakai. He brought himself back to the moment and allowed himself to take a few extra deep breaths as he focused upon Sakai. At first his voice felt weak but then it came back, "Yes, Sakai-san I am good, a little bruised but nothing too bad, you could say the wind has been knocked out of me a bit, but apart from that I'm good" Ronin replied as he coughed to clear his lungs. He pushed himself off the ground until he could stand. It took a minute or two to steady himself and then shouted over "Right, I better see if there's a way of getting you across Sakai-san"

"No problem Bailey-san, I can't see any way of getting over, maybe we need to see if the entrance way will reveal an answer to this mystery as we've got this far, what do you think?" Sakai answered as he moved forward towards the edge but keeping back enough not to slip to see if there was any clues that presented themselves to him. He looked but could see nothing. Ronin turned towards the carved doorway that was in the middle of rock face. He could see a smaller gap in it like the other ones. He thought that maybe there could be some kind of slot that he could fit in the Tsuba.

Then he saw it, a small notch where he could fit it. He reached down into the small haversack on his side and removed the Tsuba from it. He lifted it up, but this time, there was something different about it, it seemed to vibrate, he could hear a humming sound emulating from it. Ronin positioned it within the small gap and pushed forward as it clicked into place. Nothing happened at first, but then he heard several clicks and a rumbling was heard as though gears were clicking into place. He turned around to face Sakai as the ground in front of him started to vibrate and then he saw it. There seemed to be a bridge pushing out of the rock face just beneath the edge. It continued until it reached the far side where Sakai stood and then there was a series of clicks and a loud thud as it stopped moving. Ronin continued to look at Sakai, unsure what to even say at first and then the words appeared within his mouth "Well, I think we can safely say we've found a way across Sakai-san" Ronin said with a wry smile upon his face. Sakai gave a slight chuckle as he stood speechless at first. "Yes, I do believe you are quite correct Bailey-san" as he stood looking at the bridge ahead of him. Ronin stepped forward as he moved towards the edge of the chasm that was nothing but black, nothing beneath except a deep void. He looked ahead at Sakai and started to step towards him. He placed his foot upon the bridge. It was definitely not rock that was beneath his foot, he shone his head torch upon it and he could see that it was actually some kind of metallic surface he could see. "What say you Sakai-san, do we take another leap of faith? I guess this was installed for the worthy or something. I have to admit that something entirely different happened when I approached that last doorway, it was as if the Tsuba was returning home or something as it began to vibrate and give off a slight hum as it got closer to the doorway mechanism. I'm not even sure what to make if that to be honest. Maybe this is truly the true entrance to Hanzō's tomb" Ronin said as he shone his head torch a little further ahead of himself as he placed another foot upon the bridge.

Sakai looked directly at Ronin, a little shaken but more with the possibility of what could lay ahead. He wasn't sure even to make of what had happened but he was willing to believe that everything that had happened had done so for a reason. "Bailey-san, I think you are quite correct. Only the most cunning of warrior would have made it this far. I think you can safely say that you have proven yourself to this point. The last few hours has been nothing short of unbelievable to be honest with you. I'm not even sure what to make of it. I have faith that this isn't a trick to fool the worthy and to collapse deep into this chasm beneath. I trust you Bailey-san. You have truly shown your truth worth and spirit. Let's make this last part of this journey and find out what lays ahead together" he replied as he placed his right foot upon the metal bridge beneath him. He had to put all his true faith in his own footsteps and continued to move forward, literally one step at a time until he reached the far edge where Ronin was standing. He took a massive exhale of breath, only then did he come to realise that he had been holding it in true interpretation of what he was facing. As he stepped forward in front of Ronin and just looked at him.

Ronin broke the silence "Come on Sakai-san, we haven't come this far to be standing looking at each other, let's see what all this is all about, but firstly can I have my pack back please" he said. It wasn't until Ronin had said that, that Sakai realised that he had been gripping tightly his pack. The long pack that had fitted upon Ronin's back was about a metre long and he had a fairly good idea of what was inside it. To him, it reminded him of a hard sword case but instead of side clips, there was one place at the top of it which a groove ran around it, he could only guess that was the opening to it. He lifted it up and passed it over the Ronin, who held that wry smile. "Thank you Sakai-san, this is indeed precious to me, you have probably guessed what is inside it. But luckily I haven't had to use it yet and let's hope I don't have to. Now let's see what's behind this doorway shall we?" He asked as he began to turn around to face the doorway ahead of them. He stepped forward until he reached the place where he had fitted the Tsuba. He placed his hand upon it and still he felt a slight vibration through it. He started to turn it until he heard another click. He then heard something that sounded like cogs moving behind the wall until he heard a solid thud. Then the doorway built into the rock face clicked and silence. He removed the Tsuba and placed it back in his haversack. He turned and stepped towards the doorway, but something was different about this one. He felt a draft of cool air upon his face which he thought was strange as they were underground and that would only mean that there was an opening somewhere that the air was flowing into. It hadn't felt that they had started to walk back up towards the surface. As they had reached a little way into the first chamber or cavern, it had felt a little like they were descending and then moving into the second, it was like it was a slight curve up but he had thought it was his mind playing tricks with him. He put all these thoughts to one side as he looked at Sakai-san. "Let's see what all this about shall we?" For the first time, Sakai felt confident that they were truly onto something, he looked at Ronin and simply replied with a confidence in his voice that he had not spoken with in years "Let's see what the gods of destiny have laid in front of us, only we are the true masters of our fate, we haven't come this far to fail. Every step has led us to this moment. Let's take it as we see it and allow the winds of evolution guide us towards this final path" he said as he stepped forward alongside Ronin instead of behind him.

CHAPTER TWENTY-ONE

The doorway revealed a smaller chamber, a lot smaller than what they had experienced before. Shining their head torches around, the light reflecting off the walls, ceiling and floor. It only measured about 10 metres long, wide and tall. A perfectly measured and constructed square room, walls smoothed to an almost mirrored effect, going off the glint from the head torches. Ronin wasn't surprised that this room or chamber, for which he would say that was more what it was like. As he realised travelling through these caverns, they became smaller and less rough. They really seemed like travelling through a womb into the outside world. But for now, they both just moved their heads left and right, from top to bottom and never spoke for a good few minutes as they took in the beauty of this particular chamber. It was very simplistic in its design. There were carved figures situated on both sides of the path that made its way towards a shrine of some kind, that in its self was positioned behind what looked like a eloquent coffin which stood at least 5 foot from the ground. When Ronin shone his head torch upon the figures, he could make out some facial features but wasn't sure until he had gotten closer to inspect them. All he was concerned with was the fact of whether the room was booby trapped in any way.

Ronin faced Sakai and for the first time, he could see a moment of elation upon his face. He wasn't sure what was even next or what to even expect but he did have his doubts as he kept asking himself "Would Hanzō make it this straight forward? Surely there was more to it than this?"

Ronin broke the silence "What say you Sakai-san? My heart is hoping this is it but my head is believing that there is more to this than everything we've faced. Do you really think Hanzō would have made it this straight forward?" He asked as Sakai looked at him in complete contemplation before answering "Bailey-san, I think you are quite correct in your thoughts, yes I do believe to even get this far, Hanzō wanted to make sure only the greatest of warriors would make it this far but to be worthy of getting anywhere near his blade, well I think there is definitely more to come. But for now, even entering this chamber it feels different. Almost as though we've reached some kind of respectability earned from Hanzō. I can't see any kind of imminent danger but we do have to make sure we're taking every precaution. Shall we walk this path together?" He replied. Ronin nodded in agreement. The path they had taken so far had pushed especially himself to a level of discomfort that he hadn't faced in many years and he had some doubts, but apart from that he knew that they were definitely a lot closer to the truth than what they had experienced before. He knew that even if they got past this point, they still had to face whatever Yamada was going to throw at them, whether that was Higanbana or a small army. He thought it was a shame that all signal had been lost from the motion detectors that he had set up on the path towards the entrance. In some way that would have given them some kind of advantage. But then again, once they were in open air, he would be able to pick up some kind of signal. Even though he wasn't even sure how far they had travelled away from their original location. He looked around for one last time and decided that it was now or never. The pathway looked fairly even and wasn't like anything previously they had walked upon. He inhaled deeply and stepped forward, waiting for whatever was going to be presented to him.

As he did so, Sakai took a deeper breath but in surprise as he didn't expect Ronin to act there and then. He watched as he stepped forward, for a split second it looked as though he was taking another leap of faith and time slowed down. He was going to say something but his body refused to act and so he watched, waiting patiently as Ronin started making his way forward until he stopped, aligned opposite the first set of statues that they had tried to inspect with their head torches. He slightly held his breath, waiting.

"So far, so good Sakai-san. There doesn't seem to be any kind of traps or surprises but I'm not ruling them out. Even though I've taken every precaution, you should still tread carefully when you walk. But this is very interesting" Ronin said as he stood indicating with his head at the statue that he was standing opposite. "Why's that Bailey-san? Does it explain anything at all?" Sakai asked. Ronin turned his face towards Sakai and replied "Come see for yourself" but for some time, Sakai could see that he said that with a slight grin. He decided it was definitely now or never for himself as he stepped forward and his foot touched the first slab, he felt as though he didn't even want to put any pressure on them, he still allowed himself to put some pressure upon it. As he made his way towards Ronin, he still had some anxiety of what possibly could happen. But then it dawned upon him as that was what this journey so far was about. Maybe it's about being in a state of consciousness to expect the unexpected but still to enjoy the process of the journey. As he made his way towards Ronin, he lifted his head up to fill the space ahead of him with light that also fell upon the statues. The deep indentations and grooves that made up the face revealed the masks of an ancient samurai. As he shone his head torch from one statue to another, he could see that they were very similar in their appearance. He looked at Ronin, if this was what he was thinking than Ronin would agree with him. "Do you think these are exactly what we think they are Bailey-san?" He asked. Ronin took a moment in thought before answering. "Yes, I do believe what we are looking at here is part of Hanzō's guards. The ones that would protect him in the afterlife. If these are the ones that are clearly mentioned in the ancient texts, then this is truly Hanzō's last resting place. It does mention 12 warriors that stood silently over the resting place of the last master. And if we are correct, then that over there is indeed Hanzō's true coffin" he said as he pointed towards the stone mound situated at the end of the cavern. He turned towards it and pointed his head torch, allowing the beam to shine upon the risen stone coffin, surrounded by what looked liked candles that had melted and dripped down the sides, giving it a shine when the beam hit them. "Now, let's get this done, after coming all this way, I actually want to get out of here as much as I want to stay" Ronin said as he stepped forward. He had no concerns that there was any more traps as the texts mentioned nothing, but that could also change. As he approached the stone coffin, he could see multiple carvings along the sides and top of the coffin. As he went to run his hand across the top of it, he started to feel a slight vibration through his hand. He shone his head torch across the top and then bent down to run it along the sides looking for any kind of way of opening it. He spent a few minutes studying the coffin before the silence was broken by Sakai. "Is there any way of getting into there without breaking the seal with our crowbars? I don't want to cause any damage to it at all" he said as he watched Ronin study the exterior of the coffin. Ronin stopped and rubbed his hand over a section on the side that seemed to be filled with dust and molten wax. He then slid his hand down to his ankle and pulled out a thin blade. Sakai stood slightly surprised of what kind of protection Ronin had brought with him, if that blade went by anything. He watched as Ronin slid the blade into the grooves and carved out the dust and wax, when he had finished he put the blade back and then slid his hand into the haversack containing the Tsuba which he had removed. He turned and faced Sakai with a grin upon his face "If this is what I think it is, then the Tsuba should reveal for the last time what we've come here for" he said as he aligned the Tsuba into the gap and pushed it in. He waited and then heard a click and a thud as a locking mechanism activated. He stood up and placed his fingertips under a slight rim of the coffin. "If you take the other side Sakai-san, then we should be able to lift this or at least slide it down to reveal its contents" Ronin said as he nodded towards the other side. Sakai made his way round and positioned himself opposite Ronin, sliding his fingertips under the exact opposite of

Ronin's. Ronin looked at Sakai and said only one word "Ready?" Sakai felt a rush of adrenaline flow through him that he had not felt for years. "More than you'll ever realise" Sakai replied as started to lift the top at the same time as Ronin. What was inside could possibly reveal one of the greatest Japanese archeological discoveries of its history. As they lifted the lid, Ronin felt the vibrations get stronger as he revealed more of what was beneath. He held his breath as they had to move the lid backwards, only when they had taken it back far enough did he exhale a breath as deep as his thoughts of what looked at him deep within the coffin.

CHAPTER TWENTY-TWO

The coffin seemed to be filled with light with the amount of sparkles that reflected off what lay beneath. Ronin had to turn his head for a moment, he never expected to be met by such a blinding light from such a dark place. He tilted his head slightly and looked into the coffin as the beam of his head torch allowed him to gain some light. The curvature of the skull was like nothing else, a demon staring back at him projecting fear into his mind. Ronin blinked a few times as he had to look a few times, even if he knew exactly what he was looking at now, it still took him by surprise. He looked again and realised that when he originally looked, his head torch had literally bounced off small crystals that had been placed there. What he saw ahead of himself was something that he had seen many times over his lifetime. It was a Men-yoroi, what is commonly known as a Menpō or Mengu. Japanese samurai facial armour worn by both the samurai class and their retainers in feudal Japan. The different types include sōmen, menpō, hanbō or hanpō, and happuri. Not only was it work to protect their face but also instil fear into their enemies in combat. There are many different designs, some with added moustache, fangs and detachable nose. Ronin had seen it on display in both his own fathers residence as a child to many other places. He was taken back by the scattered crystals but he was sure they had been added to create an illusion of blinding light and then terror as anyone shining any kind of light within would experience.

Sakai had not even said any words as he stood there, almost in a state of shock for what he had seen. Not only had he experienced that same moment of panic as Ronin, but also excitement when he saw what really lay beneath. He had spent all his around these sets of armour and yet they still fascinated him all these many years later. "So what say you Bailey-san, you think this is Hanzō? One of the greatest warriors of all time" said Sakai as he looked at Ronin.

Ronin was still looking, still contemplating all the thoughts, analysing, not only the sight that presented itself to him below but Sakai's words. "You indeed could be right Sakai-san, we won't be 100% sure unless we remove this lid and take full stock of what we are looking at. There surely is some kind of answer to all this, I don't think we came all the way here to fail and I'm sure our enemies who want the same prize will disagree with our thoughts if they were in the same place we were standing. But let's remove this lid first and then we can take a moment to really know, heh Sakai-san" he replied. "Yes, you are right Bailey-san, let's get this lid off and then we will know" Sakai replied as placed his fingers under the rim of the lid, preparing himself to lift and reveal all.

"On the count of three, we lift and shift this, ok Sakai-san?" Ronin said, looking at Sakai, who replied with a simple nod. "Three, Two......One and liiiiiiiffft" Ronin said as he took nearly the full strain of the lift of the lid as Sakai was at an age where he would not be returning from this crypt if anything happened to him now. Together, they lifted the and brought it to rest against the wall next to the coffin. After a few moments of replenishing their lungs, they both looked at each other, both men looked wondering what thoughts were going through each other's minds.

Ronin turned and looked fully at the coffin beneath him. Within lay, a full samurai armour, almost perfect. The only difference was that the arms were resting upon the chest and within its gloves, it was grasping something. It looked as though they should be holding a sword but nothing was there, it was an empty gap or so he thought. He leaned forward and took a closer inspection, he reached forward to touch the armour. As he went to touch it, he felt waves of vibration making its way off the armour. He couldn't understand how this was even possible. But he still moved his hand forward until it touched the gloves which were cold to touch. What he thought was empty space lay something within its grasp. He rubbed the space to remove the thin layer of dust. What lay underneath his hands was something hard and rough in places but as he shone his head torch upon it, he could see a definite shape. He looked up at Sakai which seemed a lifetime since he last spoke "Do you think it is what I'm thinking it could be Sakai-san?" He asked. Sakai had been as mesmerised as Ronin as he watched him get closer. He had thought the same, maybe even about nothing being there. It seemed like an illusion was presenting itself but as whatever had prevented them from viewing the object, that had been removed and he could clearly see what looked like an oblong shaped item. About 9 inches long, it certainly looked like a katana handle or otherwise known as a Tsuka but he wasn't entirely sure. He just looked back up at Ronin and spoke whatever he had thought first "I do believe you are quite right Bailey-san, it is the right length and shape to be a handle or otherwise known as a Tsuka. Even the intricate weaved pattern of material to form a grip is still intact, but my biggest question is only simply of where the rest of it is. But there is only one piece we need to see to fully originate this as what we think it is. Have you got the Tsuba Bailey-san?" He asked. Ronin reached around and slid his hand within his haversack and pulled out the Tsuba, he brought it up and started to position it in the place where it should be, even as he did that, he could feel the vibrations intensifying as it got closer. It almost gave off this magical intensity as if it was meant to be. As he positioned it where it should naturally sit under the handle base and between the blade, there seemed to be an indentation or groove that had been made with it over time, the leather had formed a shape to allow it to sit. Now it seems as if this became part of a bigger mystery. If the Tsuba had been fitted on there, then it must of been sitting there some time before being removed to have made that indentation, which means that whoever had removed both the blade and Tsuba a good while after it had originally been placed there, possibly in the region of the last hundred years. But Ronin decided that he wouldn't mention that part to Sakai yet. He needed to know what they would do next, which presented itself when he shone his head torch upon the lower end of the Tsuka and saw what looked like a rolled up piece of paper. He looked up at Sakai and decided to at least say something for now "It does most certainly look like it is the Tsuba that fits this sword, and if this is Hanzō's sword, then this is most certainly Hanzō himself. The biggest question we face is where is the blade? I would say that this was a complete piece up to about a hundred years ago going off the indentation upon the leather breastplate. But it does seem like we've been given a lucky break Sakai-san. There seems to be a piece of paper slid into the bottom of the handle. It'll take a pair of tweezers to remove it, especially as I don't want to damage it, hold this please" Ronin said as he handed over the Tsuba to Sakai. Ronin reached into a pocket and removed a pair of tweezers, as he positioned them next to the paper and began to grip it. He didn't want to damage it, as he applied pressure upon it, he started to pull back and began to remove it, the paper slid out until it was fully free of the Tsuka. He used both hands to unroll the paper which was stiff with age but upon unrolling it, he could see there was some kind of illustration upon it. It looked like another kind of map, as he shone his head torch upon it. He could see what looked like another set of mountains, much like what had been illustrated on the original map. Ronin took a few moments to compare the various illustrations and looked up at Sakai. "Well, I think if I'm correct Sakai-san, this does show another mountain but this time it's slightly different from the ones we saw upon the original map. If I'm correct in thinking, these circles are more closer together, which means it's taller and the tallest mountain in all of Japan is Mount Fuji. This would make sense of why Hanzō chose this mountain to lay the blade to rest here. What do you think Sakai-san?" He asked whilst looking back at the map. Sakai had stood thinking all the time Ronin had been talking, all his thoughts were fixated on the idea of what this blade would look like. He couldn't believe that he was here standing in front of one of Japan's greatest warriors. It was as if Ronin was simply taking it in his stride and if he had bigger thoughts, he certainly wasn't showing them, well not to him. There was only one thought going through his mind and that was that even if the blade was upon Fuji. They had to get out of this cave before it became their final resting place and yet what was awaiting them outside, as Higanbana was surely waiting for them to take the prize away from them. They hadn't even thought of what they were going to do with what lay in front of them. Here lay one of Japan's greatest warriors and yet there was no way they would be able to remove anything as there were too many ancient curses attached to items that lay in front of them. He made his decision fairly quickly. He knew that Ronin would agree with him but it was the right decision to be made as he looked at him.

CHAPTER TWENTY-THREE

"I personally think that time is certainly against us Bailey-san. Even if we do get out of here, there is that possibility that Higanbana will be waiting for us to show ourselves. They will be ready to take whatever we've discovered. If the blade is laying upon Fuji, then we mustn't lead them there. We have to firstly find a way out of here that will evade them. Yamada will be awaiting for us to walk straight into a trap of some kind. How will we even get out of here, plus even if we do, then to disappear that will take some feat without avoiding Higanbana. Let us replace this lid and decide what's next. Hanzō would never have created this place without a second entrance or in this case, it'll be an exit" Sakai said looking at Ronin the whole time. Ronin knew that he was right, Yamada would not be allowing them to leave here with the prize. He knew that once they had surfaced then he would be able to get a better understanding of what was surrounding them. If he thought back on what intelligence he knew of Higanbana, then there would be a good handful of his men with him who would do whatever it took to complete the mission. He was pretty sure that the sensors he had set up around the entrance would pick up any traces of them and alert them early enough. The good part was that this area in which they were situated was a distance away from them, so at least that was an advantage. But all this time, his thoughts were on how they were even going to get out of here. If he was right, then recalling what was on the map. There seemed to be some kind of description on the cave in which they stood. It spoke of the 'Dragons Mouth' whatever that was. He looked around him and shone his head torch upon the walls that surrounded them until it landed upon an area behind them. He could make out something carved out of the wall, to him, it looked like a symmetrical shape that curved down towards the floor. When he moved the head torch around that area, he could see something there, but he wasn't quite sure.

"Sakai-san, can you shine your head torch onto the left section of that wall whilst I illuminate the right hand side? I think if we work together on this, we'll get a better view" Ronin said as he stood back a moment. Sakai didn't say anything at first as he understood exactly what Ronin was asking. As he positioned himself to the left of the coffin and if Ronin, he allowed his head torch to cover a good section of the wall. There was indeed grooved sections on it, but more importantly it wasn't there as a natural occurrence. He held his breath as what lay ahead of him started to reveal itself to him, he exhaled as it presented itself to him "You're right Bailey-san" was all he said as Ronin had shone his head torch upon the right hand section and then together as they illuminated the wall, the grooves started to make sense. What lay ahead of them was a dragons face, quite a majestic one at that. The grooves had been carved out of the rock face to create the scales and as they flowed down towards the floor, he could see that it created an open mouth. "Quite some work don't you think Sakai-san? Now let's see if this is indeed an exit for us, but first, let's get this coffin sealed. Hanzō has indeed answered our questions and ready to lead us to the final part" Ronin said as he moved back towards the coffin lid. He positioned himself next to it whilst awaiting for Sakai to do the same. Sakai had joined him and together they lifted the lid, which they did in silence. A simple nod and they moved it back until they had positioned it over Hanzō's coffin, they lowered it but left a gap revealing Hanzō's head. The crystals sparkled bright as the light bounced of them.

Ronin had never expected to see such sights on this journey but some sights make an impact more powerful than you'll ever imagine. The mask he saw in front of him reminded him of the ones he saw as a child adorned upon the various suits of armour that his childhood home had situated around it. It also reminded him of the mask he had worn his whole life. The one of a man who had fought the evils of this world and yet found himself fighting himself at every step. Underneath that mask he wore was the face of a man who had been broken so many times and rebuilt himself a thousand times. Every life he had taken had sacrificed his soul a little more each time till it was blackened a little more. There were times he had stopped and pondered whether he had a soul left, especially after fighting his father. That last strike had been one he had never wanted to take but yet he knew that he had taken it for so many reasons. To end a tyrant, a soul so corrupt that it wouldn't have travelled to the land of their fathers and rested well. Tanaka had caused so much hurt and destruction and yet it had been Ronin's destiny to end such damage. He had tested himself so many times throughout this journey and yet he questioned his morals but he knew that the answers lay in his actions what he would do today. The blade that they had come searching for was hid way above the clouds and yet the armour that lay in front of him was what they had actually come to find in some ways. This was proof that Hanzō had been buried in his own place away from the one destination that many thought he had been buried. It answered so many questions that many had asked. Ronin knew he still had a fight on his hands and he was prepared to take that final fight to Higanbana if need be. It was time to end this madness, especially if Yamada wanted what they had possessed.

He looked up at Sakai and nodded "It's time Sakai-san, we've come to find the truth and yet it lays right in front of us, but yet we need to travel far above the clouds to end this journey. I suggest we leave Hanzō's Tsuba where it lays, where it belongs. We have no right to take it and yet I feel we should take it and bring the three pieces together for once and for all, but yet if we do then Yamada will hunt us till the end of the earth, using Higanbana to do his bidding. What say you?" He said, awaiting the answer he knew that was coming.

Sakai knew the answer he should be giving and yet something else was directing his mind to other thoughts. He wasn't sure if it was the answer that Ronin would agree with, but he knew he would have to at least let it out. He looked at Ronin with a look of empathy as he knew what he was thinking. "You know the answer that I'm going to give, but I'll be honest with you Bailey-san. I think we should take the Tsuba and Tsuka with us, unite the three pieces together and lay them together on the top of Fuji. No greater monument to Hanzō, bury them together and allow the pieces to never be raised again. I don't want them to be taken and abused to gain a tyrant like Yamada more wealth from something that doesn't belong to him like he's done so many times. If we leave the Tsuka here, then Yamada will force his way in and destroy what's here. Let's leave Hanzō's body to be at peace that he's entitled to. Yamada has no respect for the living or dead and yet he's been making money off them for years. He's built his legacy upon them. He manipulates people like Higanbana to gain greed whilst many suffer. At least if we take the two pieces that we have, we can have some control over their future" Sakai said as he knew he was doing the right thing but at the same time he understood that sometimes you have to do what's not always right but morally it is if it means that something sacred is protected.

Ronin knew that Sakai was right, deep inside he didn't want to see Yamada gain more wealth from other people's suffering. He did know that they were taking a chance and yet it was the best chance they had of securing Hanzō's legacy would be protected. He was ready for that fight that was waiting for them. He wasn't prepared to see Sakai in harms way, he was fully prepared to do that himself. He would go first into battle as that was his destiny, his own legacy created since he was born.

"You're right Sakai-san, let's go" was all that Ronin said as he slowly removed the Tsuka from Hanzō's grip. As he did, he whispered a Haiku from Matsuo Basho;

Natsu kusa ya,
Tsuwamono domo ga,
Yume no ato

Summer grasses,

all that remains,
of warrior's dreams

With that, he nodded at Sakai and positioned his fingers under the rim of the lid which Sakai did himself, and on a count of three, they slid the lid back on until a loud thud was heard. They both released a slow breath of relief as they stood back and allowed the moment to pass. Ronin spoke in a low tone and Sakai knew what was coming "Let's get out of here Sakai-san, the journey is going to be dangerous but worthwhile" Ronin said as he stepped forward towards the doorway that was carved in the wall ahead. He held the Tsuba his hand and lifted it into a slot that was in the wall. As he fitted it in, he heard a thud of working parts moving and felt the wall move as he placed his hand upon a doorway that appeared in the wall. He pushed and a crack appeared to reveal a passage-way ahead.

CHAPTER TWENTY-FOUR

The passageway was narrow and yet Ronin felt as though he was walking through an enlarged room. His mind was feeling expanded, he thought maybe it was everything they had experienced in the last few hours that had made him feel that way. As he used his hand to make his way through the passageway, he felt as though he was slowly making his way upwards due to the air changing around him. He had never felt more prepared for anything than he had now. He knew what faced them and what he had to do, maybe it was just the adrenaline slowly coursing through him that made him feel this way. As he progressed forwards, he did feel as though the air was getting lighter, he seemed to be able to breath deeper as he made his way forwards and upwards. He could feel himself mentally preparing for what lay ahead and what was to happen. Maybe it was years of practice, but this time it felt different. As they made their way up, he sensed Sakai behind him but he was sure he felt a lightness around him as though he too was cleansed of all that had happened. Ronin stopped as soon as the passageway widened slightly, he wasn't sure but it did seem as though there was some indication that there was some natural light ahead and yet it seemed like a lifetime that they had been underground. He had lost all track of time whilst they had been down here, so he wasn't even sure what time it was. He knew that Sakai was behind but turned to speak to him "You all good Sakai-san? The path here seems to be getting wider and yet that only means one thing and that is we are soon to be returning to the surface. I only hope that we will be returning back to a point that will allow us to gain some kind of advantage over Yamada's troops, especially as we both know that Higanbana is going to be there. I really want to get a head start on them and I hope that we've made enough of a distance away from them to allow that. As soon as we reach the surface, I should be able to get some kind of signal from the sensors I placed around the original path. If anyone has tried to follow our tracks, then it would have picked them up. I'm not going out there without my backup though" he said whilst reaching to the side of his body and unclipping the pack he had on his back, allowing it to slide off.

Sakai had said very little as he knew that now was Ronin's time and that he would rather allow him to do what he needed to do. He would just follow him. He had gained a lot of trust in him over the last few hours with everything they had gone through and yet he felt calm enough to completely trust him.

He had never felt like that around anyone else for a long time. He felt compelled to speak but it seemed like the words wouldn't come at first. "You must do what you feel is right Bailey-san, I trust your judgment and allow you to create the pathway ahead. I shall simply follow" he said. A calmness had passed over him like nothing before. He watched as Ronin unclipped the pack that he had removed off his back. He had a good feeling of what was inside but watching him with his own eyes remove several items secured those thoughts for him. He watched as Ronin slowly assembled a sword that was a good length and then placed it down upon the floor as he closed the case and slung it across his back to secure back in place. But then he did something he was not expecting, he lifted his arm up and watched a blade extend from his wrist and then retract. He swallowed deeply as he was not expecting that. He wondered how many more weapons he carried and knew enough about him that he did not use any kind of firearm.

It was if the eagle soared high above, watching its prey moving and hiding, slowly moving away from its vision. Eyes on the target and yet they never blinkered from that advantage point. But yet the eyes were not of a bird but that of a human. They scanned the area in front, watching and waiting for their prey to make a mistake. They had already targeted ten shapes below, ready to eliminate when the time was right. They knew what had to be done and yet they had no fear in the task that lay ahead. Those words "Protect them at all costs, beware of the false sibling destined to gain a false crown" were burned into their memory. All this time and yet they thought they knew the answer to the question. To them, Ronin had always been the threat and one which in their mind was always a mighty opponent. But since he heard them words, they had been spending a lot of time questioning what they thought they knew and not what may actually be the truth. They had spent a lifetime waiting for the opportunity to destroy the one person who had changed everything. Their father had been someone they had grown to look up to and admire, but now they had so many doubts in their mind. They thought that maybe everything had lost that sense of reality. When they looked again through a magnified lens to target their prey in front, it was easy pickings. Especially from this height. They could easily dispatch at least five of them without anyone even knowing the placement of their ending. But what troubled them most and that was they had no fear of the smaller threats that could be taken out without a doubt, it was the real target in front, the one who changed everything. They thought that maybe, just maybe this was the false sibling of which they were told and warned off. This they were not so sure about as they scanned the ground below. They knew that there was something that had changed with them words. They pushed all thoughts to one side and focused on the task below. A little quote floated around their mind "Some days change nothing, whilst the days that change everything are not the ones you thought they were" They thought for a moment and maybe today was that day but who knows.

Ronin made sure of the rest of his kit as he readied it. He had decided to sheath his sword for now on his back, he had enough weapons at his disposal for now. He had been mentally preparing for what may lay ahead. They had stopped a good twenty-five metres before the entrance of this passage. For they were not sure where it came out as the direction they thought it may have been, might actually be taking them back in the direction they wanted to avoid and to make an easy escape. For they had found themselves being taken around a sloping pathway which seemed to winds itself like a tail of that dragon.

As they approached the entrance of the cave, they slowly made their way to make their way into daylight. The day itself was slowly dying as the dusk crept in upon them. At least one thing Ronin was pleased about and that was that he was able to utilise night vision. He had an advantage over the situation and that he may be able to change it. He reached up and allowed his hands to grip the edges of the rock face as he made his way forward. Sakai was just behind him, they had decided it would be best to take it slowly leaving the entrance of the cave. Working together, they could get a better understanding of what was in front of them. As they got to the last possible area in which they were concealed from sight they stopped and scanned the ground in front of them. Ronin knew by the terrain that they faced that it was open ground and yet he had checked the sensors that he had placed on the path into the entrance of the cave. The readings on his wrist computer showed that there was some movement about six hours ago at the last count, what it was he wouldn't be able to tell. It could have been an animal of all things. What he didn't want was to leave this entrance and face an enemy that he would have to fight through. He knew that they would be decked out in NVG's and have rifles with laser finders and silencers attached. He spent a few moments watching the vast ground ahead. There was only thing for it and that was to send up a mini drone to get a better advantage over what lay ahead. According to their GPS readings, they were about two hundred metres away from their original positions from the cave entrance. He knew that if they made any kind of movement into the ground ahead, then they would be easy targets. To leave this position and head out would mean they could be easily compromised but he didn't want to see Sakai put in any danger as he wouldn't be able to fight his way out of this. It was like a dangerous game of predator and prey. He reached into a pouch attached to his side and pulled out a mini drone. Once the drone was in flight, he could have a better overview of what was out there, ideally he wanted them to move out and head in a northern direction to get back to a safe location where they could meet up with transport they could call on to get them out there. He switched on the drone, allowed it to warm up before sending it into flight above the ground. Any signals below would show up as heat sources. Sakai had placed himself next to Ronin, saying nothing, he didn't want to put himself in a position where sound carried across the ground ahead. He watched as Ronin pressed a few switches and buttons on his wrist computer. All he could do was wait and see what was next.

Ronin watched on the small screen as the drone carried out a sweep of the ground below. There was minimal return of what was below. Nothing showed on the screen, but as Ronin knew that nothing would show up this close to this rock formation. If anywhere, they would be positioned further back to allow him and Sakai to fall into a lull of false security and allow themselves to become compromised. Ideally, the direction they wanted to head in was straight ahead, back towards they came. But then something changed, the screen showed several different shadings of colours surrounded by black. The drone's camera had heat sensors and an array of various other sensors attached, but Ronin hoped that he would get a good view of what lay ahead before they picked up that they were being spied upon and take evasive actions. Out here with silenced weapons, there wouldn't be anyone that would be reporting it to any kind of law enforcement. The way they were spread out in an arc meant that even at the very edge of the ground, there was a possibility that they would be detected. Just when Ronin was going to send the drone into a another sweep of the ground below, the sky erupted into light and the pinging noise of silenced weapons. It seemed to bring a new dawn as the light covered an arc ahead of them and then fall back into darkness. At least one thing that Ronin knew, that was not them making a mistake, it was a show of force to show them what awaited them.

CHAPTER TWENTY-FIVE

Ronin's mind was filled with options, he had to slow his breathing down as he went through each of them. To go forward together meant that one of them wouldn't be coming out the other side alive or he could send Sakai down the side of the mountain to get far away from danger as possible, but that meant that he would need to go forward to eliminate as many of them as possible, he wasn't even sure if Higanbana was out there or not. But what he did know was that whatever happened, he was damn sure he would take as many of them out before he met his maker. Sakai crouched down beside Ronin, he didn't want to make any kind of noise as that would only put them in danger of being discovered.

But he knew that Ronin would make the right decision as he hadn't been wrong so far. Ronin waited a few more minutes going through their options. He then made the decision he knew was right. He turned and looked at Sakai but raised his hand up slowly and pointed behind him indicating for them to move back so they were hidden from view. As they moved slowly back, they made minimal movement until they reached a safe distance from the entrance. Ronin slowed his breathing and looked at Sakai.

"So I think we know our options available for us, but I've decided the best option that's going to see us get through this or at least one of us. There's a small path to the right of the entrance you're going to take and also get the Tsuba and Tsuka as far as possible, I never want to see Yamada get his hands on these. I will create a diversion and I know that Yamada would only expect both of us to head back the way we came as the path away from the mountain is fairly rugged and it's a good twenty miles back around over some tough terrain that would slow us down, but what he doesn't know is that I've studied this area and found several paths that take you through an easier path, hidden from sight of the main plain in front. I want you to follow that path until you can get back onto the main route away from here. I know I'm asking a lot out of you but believe me Sakai-san, if Higanbana is out there, then they won't take any prisoners and those treasures will be lost forever. They belong to the people of Japan, not some ego maniac. Now take these and let's get going, we shall meet again in the place that no darkness will ever cover, I've got some hunting to do" Ronin said as he handed over the items that they had battled to recover, before he raised his arm towards the entrance ahead. Sakai was a little taken back but he knew that Ronin was right. He was a little speechless as Ronin was willing to possibly sacrifice himself for the safety of these antiquities. All Sakai could do was to nod and follow Ronin as they slowly made their way back to the entrance. When they got back to where they had reached, Ronin nodded and lifted his hand to Sakai as he indicated towards the path leading away from the entrance. Sakai smiled a strained smile as he quietly mouthed "Arigatōgozaimashita" (Thank you) and turned his head as he slowly moved away.

Ronin waited for a moment or two before he lifted a balaclava style hood over his head before taking out a set of night vision goggles and placed them upon his head, he adjusted them and flipped the tubes down over his eyes before powering them up.

Every hunter feels his prey before them, knowing that every breath may be their last. As Ernest Hemingway quite rightfully quoted "There is no hunting like the hunting of man, and those who have hunted armed men long enough and liked it, never care for anything else thereafter" Ronin had read that quote many times and many more times after he had contemplated what it was to hunt his fellow human. It questions every moral in your system and yet the outcome is still the same. He would never forget the eyes, looking into them at first to see their spirit fade and after a while he turned his head and sunk back into the night in which he appeared. For the art of the hunt is a tactical game, very much like chess and that is why he enjoyed a good game every now and again. Watching his opponent but more importantly, he watched their eyes and hands working together, just the slightest facial twitch would give them away. But now he knew what lay ahead was going to be tough, he didn't care much for guns, too crude and so he found his art in the blade. Even though he was quite a marksman, he enjoyed the presence of a sword within his hand, the flow state he reached as he swooped upon his prey silently bringing an aura of death upon them whilst their last breaths faded from them. Now it was time to find them, he knew there was at least 5-6 out there all armed with silenced weapons but that was just a mere distraction. He checked his darkened screen upon his wrist and played back the video feedback before the drone had been evaporated. It had been utilised two fold, one was to capture as much intelligence as possible on numbers but also location. It seemed that they were spread out in a typical arc at least halfway between him and the foot of the hills in front. They were making this all too easy for him as the further apart made it easier to slip between them. His only concern was either Higanbana was out there and the presence of booby traps, but he knew that he would deal with that as it came. His only goal was to see Sakai get as far as possible and get those treasures back to the people who they truly belonged to.

The wolf is never satisfied until they are hunting what's ahead of them and that's exactly what Ronin felt as he made his way towards the enemy in front, he moved as swiftly as the wind, light on his feet as he almost glided across the ground. He had to hit them hard and fast, silent and swiftly if he was going to survive this. Of what he knew, there was at least 12-15 combatants in front spread out in front of him. He crouched down and the the green blur that he saw through his NVG's gave some kind of perspective of what was in front of him. He knew if he switched to thermal, he would have a better understanding of distance. He also checked his wrist computer and saw a cluster of dots about twenty metres in front of him. But spread out enough to understand that they were not directly next to each other. That would make the task easier as he scanned the view ahead of him. He slowed his breathing down to almost nothing. As he did this, he focused on the task ahead of him. He asked himself how many times had he been in this situation and yet he knew that he had taken far too many souls in this lifetime to know that he would never be invited into the gates of heaven. He had always known that he was on a path that headed towards that spiralled path downwards. It wasn't as if he had made a conscious decision to not carry out the tasks as he knew what he had done was to increase someone else's wealth but also those he had sent to the next life would have done the same to him and anyone he was connected to. In times like this he instantly thought of Emiko, the sister he loved and yet she was the one soul that hell would not consume, he would make sure if that.

He allowed himself to refocus on the task ahead, he lifted his wrist up and with a sudden flick, a smooth blade fired upwards and then retracted as he moved his arm back down. He promised himself that if this was going to be the last hunt, then he would hunt well until he visited his ancestors. He made a quick adjustment on his wrist panel and the world in front changed to a weirdly wonderful mix of colours, he decided that as they would be operating on night vision, he would have the added advantage of switching to thermal. Whilst they would have to wait till he was close to their proximity, he would see them at a distance in all their heat patterns. He lifted himself slightly up and prepared to move, the wind would be the last sound they would hear as it carried their souls to the next life.

CHAPTER TWENTY-SIX

T he light that filled the night was one of intensity and faded as quickly as it began, the sound of sharp tinny thuds of automatic weapons filled the air and quietly rang out. The eyes that were on overwatch blinked a few times and allowed themselves to readjust to the darkness. They moved their head a few inches to concentrate on focusing through the scope that had been set up in their hide. One that they had to put together far quicker than they had wanted to, once they had known that they were on their way here to protect the one person they wanted to destroy in the world. How times change? They thought as they focused on the field below, the view was one that was commonly known as a target rich environment. Plenty of targets within one area and if timed right, they would fall quick enough for another to fall within a short time. The other scope was attached to one of the most powerful sniper rifles in the world, the L115A3 Long Range Rifle. The L115A3 long range rifle is a bolt-action sniper rifle that is chambered in .338 Lapua Magnum. It's capabilities are far reaching than ever before with an effective range of +1,100 meters. It has a stainless steel, fluted, 686mm barrel with a Schmidt & Bender 5-25x56 PM II day scope with variable 5 to 25 x magnification. Even has a Sniper Thermal Imaging Capability (STIC) thermal scope mounted forward of the day scope allows for target acquisition at night/low-light conditions, as well as being fitted with a suppressor in order to reduce muzzle flash and noise signature. With it folding stock, it makes it easier to carry in a bergan. Lastly, with its 5 round box magazine, you can cycle through targets and reload quickly.

With all this technology within their fingertips, they were able to quickly neutralise the targets in front without being seen, even though after the first few shots, they could compromise themselves so they would have to be quick to drop their targets in front. If they were in a military situation, they could have called in for fast air and drop a Joint Direct Attack Munition (JDAM) on the target, completely neutralising the targets below in one go. But unfortunately, they didn't have that reach, they would have to do with what they had. But they knew that this piece of kit would definitely do what it say it would.

As they viewed through the scope and watched their targets below as they had already scanned the area before, gaining a better understanding of what's ahead. They just needed to keep Ronin back as once he set off, there was no way of keeping him out of the line of fire and they didn't want to catch him in the crossfire. But they were confident that once they sent that first round downrange, that Ronin would stand fast and wait out. That was Ronin's typical modus operandi, wait in the shadows and strike hard and fast. They had read enough reports to know the way that he operated, but also they wanted to see him in action. Maybe allow him a few strikes before sending in the good news, they would become his overwatch.

Ronin breathed in the evening air, warm and inviting but yet what was in front of him wasn't. From what he knew, it wouldn't be an easy task. He knew he would need to move fast, taking down the multiple targets in front quickly. He had crouched into a kneeling position and started to breath slowly but consciously he knew that this was the moment that would change everything. If he was to see Sakai get away then he would have to face what was ahead of him now. He didn't want to make those choices that were presented to him but he knew it needed to be done. If they had slipped away then they would have made it so far but then they would have been hunted down for an item that would see a powerful man become far more powerful than ever before. Ronin had seen this far too many times in his life and yet that was had taken him to a dark place. Especially with his own father, the destruction he had witnessed was something he had never wanted to experience again, he had been part of that. He knew what haunted his dreams and thoughts, of all the lives he had taken, how many people had he witnessed taking their last breath and yet he had been like death themselves, facilitating such destruction. He often saw their faces visit his memory, knowing what he had done and yet there was nothing that he could done to change it. He just knew that tonight ended it. That vicious cycle was to end and yet he carried their demons deep within. He often invited death and embraced it but yet it refused to take him. He never understood that, he asked himself many times "Why can't I gain redemption for all that I've done, when does it end?" Well, he was going to change that, he was going to break that cycle, even if it meant an end of himself.

He opened his eyes and focused ahead. He switched on the goggles and saw a green hue in front. He had already scanned ahead with thermal and counted at least ten, with at least five spread out in an arc, a good distance apart from each other, both front and back. He lifted himself up and crouched ready to strike, he made his way forward, ready to commit violence to create a form of peace that even death himself would banish him from hell.

CHAPTER TWENTY-SEVEN

He saw the first kneeled down and presumed they would all be doing this. He made his way forward and swung around to face them from behind. He moved swiftly, his feet lightly touching the air as the cool night breeze sang a song of crickets, chirping and celebrating with each other. He gained distance and closed in with his target, like a hawk upon a mouse he reached out and attached his right hand upon the right side of their head, before they could react he had lifted his left and a slammed his opened left hand into their neck area, where a blade had fired forward and penetrated their neck. Without realising it, he had wrapped his body and arm around them, like a snake around their prey, silencing them and cushioning their blow upon which he placed on the earth that would become their last resting place. He looked up quickly, nothing had stirred and yet he sensed the danger around him. There would be weapons trained upon his position ahead, ready to unleash silenced death upon him in an instance. He knew they would be transmitting messages covertly and so no voice was heard from a distance. He had decided that the best form of defence was definitely attack in this instance. He scanned the area ahead of him and guessed that the distance between them was roughly twenty foot spread out but situated in a killing field with interlocking arcs so they were far enough apart to prevent hitting themselves yet would kill anyone in front.

He had switched to thermal to scan the ground ahead and seen a difference in his vision, the various colours presented themselves in front. There they were, displaying the heat of their bodies and yet they may have even picked up his own body thermals if hadn't of decided to wear thermal reduction clothing and equipment. His best move now was to strike from the rear as if he moved forward it would compromise him yet he was unsure of whether Higanbana was here. It wasn't as if he had any fear of them but it wasn't what he wanted right now. He wanted to protect Sakai so he could get as far away as possible. He saw a gap and decided to make for it which allow him to curve himself around to neutralise the rear right sentry and then take the remaining ones as they stood. He prepared himself to move when something caught his attention to the front of his position about twenty feet away, a slight rustle and then the clicking sound emulating from beneath him, he looked down at the sentry he had just eliminated and there it was again, that clicking sound, but there was a pattern to it. He knew exactly what it was and all he knew then was he had to move quickly as all he could hear was the words being spelled out in morse "To your front, on my count, in three…… two……."

Before the last word was communicated, Ronin shifted his body towards his right and away fast before the 'One' had come through and the world around him had erupted in light and tinny sounds of gunfire that sounded like a thousand crickets chirping in the summer evening.

Within a fraction of a second Ronin reacted, but so did the overwatch. With explosive movements, Ronin had moved forward and with a jolt had detached the blade from his back which he had slid forward, gripped within his hands, he had angled it horizontally and drove it forward. His target in front never knew what happened as the razor sharp blade sliced through his neck at an angle to avoid hitting his weapon he was fully focused on. What they saw in front through the concentrated flashes of deadly fireflies penetrating the darkness ahead, soon became the night sky and the stars covering the canvas above. Before their head had reached the ground, Ronin had moved from one target to another, slick controlled movements, pirouetting like a dance of death as he cut bone and sinew. But he was not the only one concentrating on raining down hell upon the earth below.

As they cycled their way through their first five targets, none of them realising that death was going to be visiting them tonight, unseen by each other as they were well spaced and within the chaos that they were directing ahead upon a suspected target. They smoothly carried out a magazine change and refocused on the targets below. Their breathing never breaking from anything but controlled, they just lined them up like bottles on a brick wall and eliminated them. All of them head shots so not to allow them to warn each other. This was their element, the words flowed their mind, that of what they had heard a thousand times "Slow is smooth and smooth is fast, fast is deadly"

As they dealt with the first line of targets, those left after Ronin had dealt with one of them, dropping each one on their first shot, they had to be mindful of where Ronin was situated, so not to be caught in the crossfire. But as Ronin reached the last target ahead, just as he lifted his sword to silence the target ahead. It was if blade and bullet had met in their collective space, Ronin watched the bullet strike the targets head and eliminate them as the blade reached it. Slightly stunned, he jolted back just as they had relaxed their finger from the trigger.

In the confusing silence that surrounded them, both of them took a moment to breath. It was if they were psychologically connected, both working from one mind. A few more moments passed and Ronin took a look around as his counterpart on overwatch scanned the killing ground below. All targets had been neutralised within five minutes, they wouldn't have had time to react to what was happening around them as they were fully focused on what they thought was ahead.

Ronin was still concentrating on his calming breaths but fully aware that he was not alone. His only thought was "Who are you? Friend or foe?" As even though they had eliminated the other targets, did they do that for Ronin to be left within the killing ground below. As he knew was he had to get far away and quickly as he wasn't even sure if Higanbana was close by or that they hadn't been here. Either ways he had to fade into the black and take his chances with the danger that he was in. He twisted his body and counted to three. Before the last e had been spoken in his mind, he leapt forward taking that chance. If he made it past the first line of targets he knew his answer.

CHAPTER TWENTY-EIGHT

They sat back and watched Ronin take flight through the scope. They had fulfilled the deal and now it was up to Ronin to finish what he had started. They had to take a few moments to evaluate what had just happened, watching Ronin work was fascinating as that's something they had never seen before, they had never seen anyone move the way that Ronin had. It was almost unnatural but all they could do now was to sit back and wait for orders of what's next. But not before breaking down their kit and extracting from here and quickly. The night would soon turn to early morning and even though they were unlikely to be comprised, they still had to get out of there. They pulled out a small iPad that had the screen darkness reduced to almost nothing, they only typed one word 'Dragon' and sent the message. They started to break down their kit and prepared to extract themselves from here. They knew that even though they may have slowed down Yamada for now, the next time they may not be so lucky as there was still Higanbana to deal with. They were something else if you listened to the rumours for not many people had actually seen them. Some would say he was a monster of a man, others would say that he was actually a shapeshifter and would appear as a slim woman. But that's what rumours are meant to do, confuse the mind and challenge your perceptions. Either way, they wouldn't want to come face to face with that kind of enigma. It was time to move and move quickly they did.

For such an impressive sight, it looked like an ice crown placed upon the rocky land. The mountain that no darkness would ever cover as it's peak would reach the gods. The one place that would determine a destiny that many had discussed but never truly discovered. The biggest question of all is once the blade is assembled, would it give the person who wielded it true power or was that just rumours as far and wide as time itself? There was only one way to find out and that was something that Ronin would do in this very moment of time as he picked up the blade and fitted the pieces together. As the last piece connected together, he held it diagonally with the blade faced towards him to show that he was not a threat and one of respect. The vibrating that through the Tsuba into the Tsuka was gaining and yet he experienced something similar on his journey, there was nothing that was starting to match this. It was growing and as he slid his hand around the Tsuka, he felt as though the light was getting brighter, he could truly understand why this was the place that darkness never covered now. But it was a massively different feeling, it was if the universe was being created right there, he felt as though it was expanding and no one knew where it would lead. He struggled to breath as the air thinned and turned into vapour. He had to concentrate on his breathing as his breathing wavered and the oxygen was being drawn out of his lungs as he brought his right hand to the centre of his body to meet his left. Once the circle had been complete, only then would the prophecy reveal itself to be true or false. But the way the light was gaining, he started to understand what it would be, but as he felt the oxygen begin to fade he wasn't so sure. He had to balance himself as he felt as though he was being drawn into a supernova, a mass explosion within the cosmos itself. The vacuum that had been created drew him in faster, his muscles burned as it forced his right arm closer to his left. So close now, his fingertips on his left hand reached out and soon they touched the Tsuba. Now to complete that circle and see what fate was going to present itself to him. He stated to see black and white squares in his vision as it became to blur. He was losing consciousness and quickly from lack of oxygen. He knew he could hold his breath for a good few minutes but even this was pushing his abilities. So close and yet so far as he pushed the Tsuka across his fingers into his palm, only now to bridge that gap. It touched the center of his palm and he fought to close his left hand around it. With every moment that passed, the light was burning out the darkness that surrounded him. Maybe his journey was over, maybe this was it. He had traveled through the darker side of life and found the redemption he was searching for as it wasn't burning him. He knew in his own mind that he had revisited that dark side so many times, but now was the time to finally change all the rules. He now gripped the Tsuba with both hands tight and awaited his destiny or fate, whatever was meant to be as the light swallowed him whole and darkness was no more.

Ronin shot up, almost in a wild panic. He was soaked in sweat and was gripping the sheets that covered him. The room was dark and the only sounds he heard was the sound of the crickets outside amongst the many insects that chatted on the evening breeze. He had to take focus of his breathing and centre his thoughts. Taking quick breaths of four seconds in and exhaling for two seconds, he repeated this for a couple of cycles until he regained his composure and relaxed his breathing. He started to take stock of his surroundings and remembered that he was in a rented apartment that he had arrived a few hours ago. To him it seemed like time had not passed at all. As he sat there allowing the cool air to pass over him, his thoughts had started to come together.

After escaping that killing field, he had made his

way through the undergrowth until he had covered almost ten kilometres to a secure location where he had left a vehicle that he could then drive to another location, this one in particular. But before he left he had made contact with Sakai, who himself had made it along the path to another secure location and transport. This had taken time and quite a fee to set up but it was worth it. As soon as Ronin knew that Sakai was safe and still had the items that could have seen them visiting the next life, he had driven to where he was now. He had rented a remote but secure apartment, far enough from prying eyes. They had both agreed that they would take a day or two to allow the dust to settle and monitor any online activities that would indicate any activities or actions taken by Yamada. The hardest part in Ronin's mind was what Yamada was doing as he was quite the illusion when it came to finding out any information of his activities, but from a few paid informants through various accounts and sources, he was able to get some good intelligence. He knew that Yamada would be raging when he found out that Sakai and him had escaped the mountain and his attempt to stop them in their tracks. But Ronin's biggest concern was not Yamada's reaction but who the mysterious overwatch was, their protector that had eliminated Yamada's men. Ronin knew that by the speed those rounds had come fired down upon them, the person sending them downrange was quite a professional in their trade, but he wondered if he would be able to find out any information about them, but that was not his primary concern right now. He threw the sheets to one side and shifted himself to the edge of the bed. The first break in dawn could be seen through the patio doors as he stood up and walked towards them. He loved this time in the morning, it was a time to feel alive. As he pushed open the doors further, he walked onto the patio and up to the balcony that overlooked the hills and forests ahead. As the morning light started breaking through, the creatures of the night started to quieten down. Ronin closed his eyes and drew in slow deliberate breaths, his mind was clearing and the breath of dawn was refreshing upon his body as he sunk into a meditative state. His next task was going to be the most difficult part. He knew that whatever came next, it wouldn't be easy neither would it be the hardest but whether he would see the end, that was the question lingering within his mind as he allowed the morning breeze to consume him.

CHAPTER TWENTY-NINE

The breath was shallow and slow, flowing but intentional. All that was within exposed itself externally. Deep thoughts that questioned the reality that all that is, isn't what may be but also the deepest thoughts are the root of all chaos. As deep as the breaths flowed so did the thoughts and flowed they did as Ronin cycled them deep within. The ones that kept cycling through his mind were the most intense realisation that death was never far from his existence, but it was something he never feared, he embraced it. To some, that would be psychological damaging but to those like Ronin that walked the path he was born into, it was certainly as easy as breathing. He struggled to understand the reasons for those that didn't respect the rule of life and why they destroyed a single life without reason. To some, Ronin was the definition of death, a wraith that blended into the dark and yet he drew upon the light. He had not killed anyone who respected life and that was what he drew upon.

That didn't stop him questioning his intentions or

reason why he had killed, it didn't keep him awake at night neither did he dislike himself for it. But he did see himself in a light that didn't shine upon all the shadows. He still kept some darkness within, maybe that was the root of the redemption he was seeking. He had made peace with himself before he stepped onto the battlefield of life and that was good enough for him. So maybe that's why he spent hours sometimes meditating, searching for the reasons of why others would allow their greed or ego infect their intentions. He had never forgotten the first person he killed. He would have only been sixteen or seventeen at the time, many years had passed since that first time. He still remembered looking into their eyes and yet he thought he saw his reflection within their pupils. The words came to him, ones that radiated through him "When death looks upon the souls of the ones that invite his cold touch, will also burn within the fires of their own destiny" Those words had stayed with him for all these years and yet he never stopped asking himself "Am I the one that's destined to walk this path with a weight of humanity upon my shoulders? Or I am the one that delivers their souls from all that infects them"

He had searched the answer to this question for many years and yet he looked at it from many angles. Maybe the truth is that he didn't want the answer, he didn't want to accept that he was the warrior that fought for the moral compass of many.

That seemed to be quite hypocritical considering the people like his own father had requested his skills to do his bidding. But he could have walked away many times but yet he looked at the ones that were painted with the hand of death and yet he saw something truly terrible in their intentions, for he could have ended his fathers reign many times and yet this is something that did weigh heavy on his mind. The more he dug and sifted, he found that he balanced the difference between the right and wrong of those that surrounded him. He had honed his skills like a fine blade, lightly balanced but deadly and a fine edge. Sharp enough to slice through the toughest rope but light enough to balance upon his index finger.

"Maybe, just maybe that's what he should have defined himself upon throughout these years?" He thought as he suddenly realised that the very weapon that he had skilled himself throughout these many years was what had directed him. The blade that was light and balanced but dark enough to snuff out the flickering flames that burned within the soul of those that feed upon the greed of their own desires.

As he cycled his thoughts through his mind, he zoned out from all in the moment. He knew that it was important to stay in the moment but only for that he was truly focused on, these very thoughts wasn't what he desired to expel his energy on. It was time to refocus on the mission, the one true motion that had brought him to this place, this chain of events that had tested his mental and physical resilience so far. He knew what needed to be done but did he really want to experience what was next? He had pondered and turned over these very thoughts. He had asked himself this very question so many times in the last twenty-four hours. He had made contact with Sakai, but instructed him to wait at the safe house before proceeding with the plan. Ronin didn't want to see him in harms way, that was his place. The part of the mystery was the identity of the sniper. He knew that he was there to protect him in some way but why? He hadn't arranged any overwatch and neither had Sakai. But it was truly appreciated. He had wondered whether it was for his protection or to eliminate the enemy to allow someone else in. Higanbana was nowhere to be seen and if they had been, maybe it would have been a very different situation. Ronin had tried to even reveal Higan-bana but to no avail. Every search had hit a wall but he knew to truly expose the truth, he would have to expose himself to the eyes that hunted the most. He decided that there was nothing to be done except keep moving forward and face his adversity with all that he believed in. If this was his true destiny, then let it be. For no man is truly mortal, unless his name is spoken after his soul ascends to the gods.

CHAPTER THIRTY

"**S**akai-san, I hope you are well my friend" Ronin said as he spoke to Sakai through the screen in front of him. "I'm very well, thank you my friend, good to see you" Sakai replied. They had linked up after a few days after making their escape from the cave. "So what's next? What's your next move Bailey-san? I take it you've got a plan in place?" Sakai said as he shifted his position to become comfortable. Ronin took a few moments to compose himself with his thoughts before answering. When he was fully ready to answer, it was like all the energy of the last few days had seeped into his mind and powered his thoughts.

"I've decided that we've reached a point of no return with this, we have what others require and for what we've seen, they will kill for it, that's a given. We have to see this through to the end. I know Yamada is fuming with this defeat from what feedback I've been getting back over the net. And I definitely know that he will send Higan-bana to do his bidding. I've searched for any intel on this mysterious person, but absolutely nothing. I still don't know anything about them and that's slightly concerning but nothing that I can't handle. All I do know is that we have to get to that blade and it's sitting upon one of the greatest mountains in the world. I've done as much gathering of intelligence as possible and by the looks of it, there's a chance that there's a crater located on the summit that by a scan taken by X-ray, there's a cavern or feature that isn't naturally occurring. It's covered by a pile of rocks which would take an hour to uncover. Talk about hiding in plain sight as thousands have made that journey and yet they haven't spoken of any differences. The only problem is that it's barren and we would be exposed on the summit. We would also need to get this done in a small window of opportunity. Now, we've got this far and we can't give up. But I don't expect you to follow me up there Sakai-san. I can take both pieces and take this final journey, for all I know, I won't return. I will unite them and bring Hanzō's secret back to the people however I can" Ronin said as the multitude of thoughts flowed through his mind as he waited for Sakai to respond.

"I can understand that Bailey-san, but I can't allow you to do this yourself. I can get a few people, skilled in certain arts to join us for protection. It will draw attention from many people including the authorities for what we're doing and that's something I don't need. Let's meet up and finalise plans to secure the final piece, I think for certain that if there's any talk over the net regarding either Yamada or Higanbana, we'll hear about it. How about tomorrow in our new location, sound good to you" Sakai asked as Ronin was taken back a little. For he had taken lead, especially to protect Sakai the best he can do, but now he saw a man step forward, full of strength of heart and mind and taking lead on a journey that will test both of their abilities, especially for a man like Sakai, for he wasn't a young man, but neither was he.

"Sounds like a plan Sakai-san, let's get prepared and get this done, for the hour is getting late and we have much to do" Ronin said as he signed off the video chat and set out to prepare himself for this last stance.

Ronin knew that no plan ever went ahead perfect the first time, as soon as you step forward then there's always going something that's going to go wrong, something completely out of your control, but that's where he knew he had some advantage. He didn't concentrate on all that he couldn't control, only what he could. One of the first tasks that he had carried out was to give himself a few days to put himself first. For he knew that no matter how good technology is, if he wasn't in prime condition, then it would fail. The apartment that he had rented was built with a fairly large room where he could train, meditate, test his kit out. He would take out each individual item and make sure it was to its optimal use, blades sharpened and oiled. He lay them out and went through each piece with care and attention. For he knew that the basics is what creates success, once you've got them down and they become your muscle memory, then you'll always fall back on that. That's something that Ronin had always believed in and instilled into his discipline and routine.

For at least a solid hour, he would spent it stretching his body, every sinew was stretched and conditioned. The years had been tough on him physically, especially the torn muscles throughout his body. He had collected quite a few scars as well, but that was to be expected. He never wanted to live a life that was left unturned or in a world where comfort was the norm. The more he had honed his body, he had found that a flexible, supple body made each day easier, but that had taken many years of discipline and putting himself in uncomfortable situations. After he had finished stretching off, he walked over to the selection of swords that he had brought with him. They were specially designed and crafted to be compact, yet functional. He loved the traditional katana, but it would never had suited him for the work he had done. As his hand wrapped itself around the Tsuka, it felt like he was home. The number of hours he had spent just practicing one movement as a child to perfect it the best he could, at first he complained aloud to his Sensei "It's too heavy" which his Sensei would reply "It is not the sword that is too heavy, it is your determination that is too weak" after that he knew that he would have to adapt to this new place of discomfort and strengthen his body so that the sword felt lighter than the lightest blade.

Every cut, stroke, pirouette, block he would practice until it flowed like the mountain river. He would train until his body was soaked in sweat and that was only for the sword work. He had always found Iaidō to be a beautiful art form, as deadly as Kendo, but as peaceful as Aikido. He had never been a massive fan of using firearms, although he was quite proficient in their use and had trained in them, that was only to have that skillset if needed. He had a love of all bladed items since a child and yet he found peace within each one he held. He never quite understood why he found it so easy to fight and move with a sword than with a firearm like his enemies. It was as though it literally did become an extension of his body. Once he had spent a good few hours spending it on the basics, then he would progress onto the essentials. But first he would cleanse his body and rest, the apartment had a sauna and cold pool which was massively beneficial to his physical and mental conditioning. Cold water therapy had become one of his main outlets to cleanse his mind as well as his body. The day was drawing to an end and as he stood watching the sun melt into the horizon, he was grateful for those moments and he always will do.

CHAPTER THIRTY-ONE

"What's your thoughts Bailey-san?" Sakai asked as he spoke through the screen. Ronin took a moment to reply as he looked at Sakai. "Well, we have everything in place so far Sakai-san, I want to keep it as simple as possible. So far, we've been using the drones to capture as much movement as possible, especially at the base and summit of the mountain. It seems to me that there's been a lot of movement of tourists which is good as we can blend in with them as we move up the mountain. It's about a 5-10 hour trek to ascend to the summit, depending on which trail we use, most people will begin from the Kawaguchi-ko 5th station which takes on average about 5-6 hours climb to the summit. This gives us another advantage as there are 4 main trails leading up to the summit of Mount Fuji, theses are Yoshida, Fujinomiya, Subashiri and the Gotenba trail. Now we know with the research we've done so far that each trail consists of a 5th station, which no cars or vehicles can progress. This is ideal as it will expose who will be on foot. Now if Yamada's men do collect and attempt to move up, they'll easily be spotted especially with the amount of kit they'll be carrying and type of kit. They may even be wearing civilian attire to blend in themselves. According to the guide books, they suggest that it's best to mingle in with the locals, and to steer away from the crowds, using the Subashiri trail. So this should be the main trail we observe. Now we also know that there are mountain huts which should at least provide us with some cover but also an advantage point to watch who's around. Now we've also got to be mindful that it does ascend to 3776m or 12,388 ft and has some serious elevation gain, rapidly changing extreme weather, steep inclines and long switchbacks. Another part we have to be mindful of is that Mount Fuji experiences some serious alpine variable weather. Even during the middle of the summer when temperatures in Tokyo reach 40c/100f, the summit of it can very well be below freezing with a biting wind. The summit can often feels like -10c/15f in the predawn chill. As the oxygen on the summit has two-thirds the density of normal oxygen at sea level which can cause altitude sickness or AMS. So not only have we got to be aware of Yamada's men but also the natural weather conditions. It's not going to be an easy task Sakai-san" Ronin replied.

They both knew that this is going to be the toughest part of the mission and yet they only had part information that the blade was at the summit.

That was based on what they had learned in the cavern, so who really knew what the truth is. They had done all the research they could and had all the kit ready. Ronin had thought that it may be worth a recce to get an understanding of the terrain and ground. Also with going off the shots that the cavern entrance is on the North West Point of the summit, they would need to gain an understanding of its position from main trails etc Ronin was massively surprised that it hadn't been discovered yet but once again, it's the old adage in play 'Hide in plain sight' If only they knew what lay under their feet, then it would be very different.

"Bailey-san, I think we've got as much intel as possible at this moment, we need to decide when best to move out as quickly as possible. Yamada will be making moves himself, who knows even if he knows our next location for only we know this. How about we do a final digital walk through/talk through and finalise the plan? Say in 2 days?" Sakai asked" He knew that they had everything against them and that wasn't just the weather. He could quite easily hire 5-10 of his own people to mix in with the other climbers. These were former Japanese military veterans that worked in the security industry and were part time consultants for the museum. That would at least balance the odds stacked against them.

Ronin knew what was at stake here and simply replied with "Of course Sakai-san, I agree that time is indeed of the essence and we need to move quickly, especially with the weather windows as well in place. We will get back together in 2 days, that will give us enough time to finalise everything we possibly can. Any questions, just send me a message, ok?" Ronin replied back. "Of course Bailey-san, not a problem, speak soon" Sakai said before signing off.

Ronin was indeed taking fate into his hands and he knew it. But he also needed to do this, especially for the truth to be revealed and to give back the sword of Hanzō back to the people.

CHAPTER THIRTY-TWO

"You need now more than ever to protect him, he's proven that he fights hard and whatever comes his way, he won't back down without a fight. We're in the process of tracking him and as soon as we do, then you'll be one step behind him, do you understand that?" The voice said as the screen illuminated the room. They sat there, lost in thought for a moment but knowing that what had been asked of them was what was necessary. They had spent countless years being told that Ronin was a threat that could bring down the whole family and now they were being asked to protect the very person who was out there to destroy it all. That was the part they couldn't understand but they took it as it come and whatever was meant to be would happen.

They focused fully on the screen and replied "But for years, father had warned me of Ronin and how he would destroy our entire family and yet I watched him that night having to step forward hesitantly raise a sword, only to prove that he never wanted to be there. That night changed everything and yet the lies shattered with that final cut. I see now that father feared that which would end his power. The man I looked up to was nothing but a bully and tyrant and feared losing that power like most tyrants. But that night I saw the pain and anguish in Ronin's face as prominent as though I had stabbed him in the heart. All these years and yet what's changed I ask you? A man who stepped out from the shadows and exposed himself to the truth, that's what changed. I'm not going to lie to you, but I have only gained respect for him. He was willing to die that night and yet he drew from his own honesty as he fought. Fathers ego and arrogance was what killed him. The crazy part is the orphan that father took on all because he saw natural talents he could manipulate for his own greed truly exposed his own lies in the end. All I need is a location and I'll be there, I'm not going to allow Yamada to take something of that much importance, only to fulfil his greed like father did for many years. Also, as for this threat from Higanbana who has been a bit of an enigma for these many years, is there any truth in them being an actual person?" They asked even though they knew a true answer may never be given.

The face on the screen had shifted themselves a little bit with the uncomfortable question being asked, but they still responded "All I know is that Yamada had sent Higanbana to wipe out one family after they had won a contract that he wanted and they didn't disappoint him. Everyone including the children and were killed that night, now one questions something though, they let the family dog go free, that is something of a mystery as it shows that they had something inside that they were not willing to step past. That doesn't make any sense but I guess nothing ever does. Who this Higanbana actually is, I guess no one will ever truly know unless they step forward. They have been steeped in mystery for many years. All I do know is that they do exist in some form. Have you got the package I sent you?" They asked whilst searching for any kind of reaction to what they had just said.

"Yes I have, but I still don't understand. You're telling me to protect someone who I've also been told for many years will destroy everything I am and what was my very foundation, why is that?" They asked.

"For that is quite simple, Ronin Bailey was quite simply a name he gave himself after he broke away from your father. Bailey was the surname of his true parents and yet he will always be a Ronin, masterless, a wanderer. For that man is closer to you than you'll ever realise. For Ronin Bailey was the adopted son of your father Kaito Tanaka which makes him your brother and you are his sister" They said and awaited the truth to be slammed upon them.

Nothing in the world would have prepared them for that to be said and it felt like he had been sucker punched. That's going to take some getting used to. All they could do was to look at the screen and reply "Now I understand, I really do, now I have a lot to do, we'll speak soon, ok?"

"Of course, you know where I am if you need me" was the only reply to an obvious question.

As they switched off the screen and the darkness swallowed them, they didn't know what to think. For all these years they had sat there never knowing the truth and to be dropped that bomb was something else. They tried to lie back and fall into a meditative state but too many questions flooded their mind. All they could do was to take the blows as they came and allow tiredness to take them to a place no one else could enter.

CHAPTER THIRTY-THREE

Preparation is the key to success, it's one of factors that determines the outcome of the event. Even down to the smallest detail left unturned will shift the way in which it will go. You can never force the direction of the flow of the events that unfold before you but you can always prepare for any eventuality and take it as it comes. That's exactly the way in which Ronin had mentally prepared himself for the next stage of the mission that he was going to begin. He had prepared his kit, both mentally and physically he was in a place which he knew that there was a chance that he wouldn't come back from but this is where he was at peace. He had accepted death a long time ago and he had fully embraced it, it was no stranger to him and he had been there before, but yet he had survived. Sometimes living by instincts alone and this is where he thrived best, within chaos. He knew that he had stepped into the realms of chaos and yet he was in full control of his emotions for he knew that these were the times in which would make or break him. He had seen many people break under the onslaught of fear that broke a person's resolution once it infected their mind.

For a couple of days, Ronin had his kit laid out in front of him. He had gone over every piece with the greatest attention and made sure it was perfect. He had chosen the equipment for the very task ahead of him but also what would work best in the conditions that he was about to step into. He knew Yamada would be sending in his men but whether he was going to send in one group or two he wasn't sure about that. He would have to wait until they were on the ground to see that. He also knew that the weather was going to be a factor that would change the flow of the task as you can never change the weather to suit it. Nothing he had ever done before made it any more comfortable by the weather. He also had to think of Sakai, he was older than him and yet he knew he was physically able enough to complete the task, that much had been proven in the caves. But he wanted him to go with the least amount of kit needed.

The footage from the drones had proven good for him as it had even picked up on the smallest details. He knew that traffic had been free flowing over this season so far, the cabins had been busy as well. All he knew was that some communications picked up over the last few days pointed in the direction that Yamada was preparing himself for something. Ronin had even tried to get some intel from some old sources but even that had gone nowhere. He had done everything to ensure that secrecy was maintained at the highest level but all it took was the slightest crack in it. He had some feedback from several sources that Yamada had sent some men into the caverns after the slaughter of his men upon that field. Of course their bodies had been removed as quickly as possible before the authorities had been tipped off but Ronin was sure that they had left as little intel that would betray their movements. Then there was that mysterious sniper, he had spent a couple of hours to try and get some intel on that but it all drew blank. They would have done everything they could to ensure their secrecy, but whoever they were, they had done their job with deadly accuracy.

Ronin had poured over the terrain of Mount Fuji, several times he had started from the bottom and plotted their course, never overlooking the smallest of switchbacks and trails. Every infiltration and exfiltration point noted and explored to ensure that nothing would hinder their journey. But when viewing the summit, there was one question that was firmly placed within his mind and that was "Why would Hanzō choose this place?" Every feasible answer that he could think of escaped Ronin's mind. He had wondered why Hanzō would have placed such a personal item or should he say hid in plain sight, knowing that many travelled upon its peak. Ronin knew that if he could gain that blade then it would never be for personal gain but for the people. Yes, it satisfied a very personal perspective as he would never want to see such a beautiful blade be left to be ravaged in that kind of environment, but it is what it is and there was nothing that he could do to change that.

All he could do was study the peak, especially that cavern. He could not believe that all these years and it had never been discovered. By the lay of the land, it was fairly well covered. He thought of all the thousands of people that had trekked that terrain and had never known about what was under their feet. Ronin knew that the cave systems that they were going to be entering will be as dangerous as any they experienced before, but once again he was prepared. All he had to focus on was making sure that they could enter the cavern without being seen. He wasn't sure even if would be possible but he knew it was worth they risk. But even that he had put a plan into place to deal with that, something of a simple one but these were the best ones. He didn't want to fill his mind with too many factors that would dent his ability to carry out the task. He knew that all was left was to get it done, without a second thought he opened up his laptop and selected an icon that would access his secure communications, he waited to be connected to Sakai and as soon as he had appeared, even before Sakai had the chance to say anything, Ronin firmly said a few words "I'm good to go Sakai-san" and he knew as soon as those words had left his mouth it was time to put themselves back into harms way and this time it was now or never.

CHAPTER THIRTY-FOUR

The gravel beneath Ronin's feet on the mountain trail was hard and cold, where it would make slippery conditions most of the year, this time there was no give and he knew that it would be even colder upon the summit. He looked around at the various people surrounding him. His eyes darted between each one, his mind constantly cycling between thoughts of just getting the mission done and whether they were going to be ambushed at any given moment. They were as prepared as they could ever have been. They had spent the early hours scanning scanning through drone feed after sending one up to get an aerial view of who and how many were there, just to get an understanding of what the amount of people were upon the mountain. Ronin knew that today felt different, he wasn't sure if it was just him being on edge or whether it was the colder conditions. He looked at Sakai and for the first time he saw a man who had seen many things within his life but nothing that would prepare him for what they were going to accomplish today.

"You all good Sakai-san?" Ronin asked, Sakai dressed in full cold weather kit was tightening his straps on his small bergan on his back. He looked at Ronin and gave a wry smile "Yes Bailey-san, as good as it's ever going to be, we have the route mapped out and I don't think it's going to get any better than this. If we are amongst the wrong kind of company, then they'll reveal themselves and then we can deal with the situation. I must admit that you surprise me Bailey-san, you have brought quite a bit of kit but yet it looks like you've concealed it well. Can I ask you whether you think Yamada has any kind of inkling of what we're intending to do today?" He asked. Ronin took a few moments, he had spent the time that Sakai was talking to study this man, there was a quiet confidence in him that he hadn't seen before and yet age wasn't betraying him. He knew of Sakai's background and that he had studied Iaido as many Japanese do. He knew that he was the right kind of person to be here today. Sakai was an impression-able person, all the research he had done on him revealed quite a character and yet he knew little about him, but that seemed to change as he spoke to him today. Ronin knew that today was going to push both of them to a physical and mental limit but he was confident that they would conquer the mountain and retrieve what they had come for. If they were going to unite the pieces together for the last time before handing them back to the people, then today was a good to do it.

"If Yamada wants to be here then I'm sure he would have put his men on the ground before now. I can't help but think that any of these people surrounding us could betray us at any given moment Sakai-san. We have done everything we can to work in secrecy, plotting false routes and creating as many diversions as possible but we must be vigilant. Especially if Yamada does have any inkling of what we're intending to do. It may be that he wait for us to retrieve the blade before falling upon us but believe me if there is any sign of an ambush awaiting us. I want you to get away as far as possible, this isn't your fight, you understand me Sakai-san?" Ronin replied in a low but stern voice. "Yes Bailey-San, I understand. My body may be getting old but my mind is still as young as ever, I think it's best to get this trek underway and we can decide upon the way on what's the best plan moving forward" Sakai replied.

The air was starting to bite at them as they set off upon the trail. Ronin knew that this was going to be a long day. He had assessed it and taken the time to get a few viewings of the traffic upon the trails over the last few days. But his biggest concern was the summit, if the cave did exist, then how were they going to gain entrance with others around them. This is going to be their biggest challenge, but yet he knew that he would just take it as it came to them. They had a long enough journey ahead of him. He knew that he wouldn't let his mind overthink but there was always something that would be ticking away in the back of it. The trail seemed to be quite steady underfoot as they made their way up it. They were both dressed in the best possible equipment and they were fully prepared to meet any kind of resistance that they met upon the way.

This was going to be the most difficult part of the journey as it would deplete them of energy to keep moving towards the summit. Ronin's thoughts were drifting between the here and now and the past. The air reminded him of a time when he was a child going swimming and the river was freezing. It was cold but yet refreshing at the same time. His thoughts were fleeting of those times but he knew that certain environments brought back memories of his lifetime, especially as a child. That day, his Sansei had told him he was going swimming in the river, Ronin looked upon him with a look of half wonder and half fear especially as he tried challenging it "But Sensei, the water is freezing, I'm going to die in there?" His Sensei chuckled, especially as he knew all children spoke in the worst case scenario. "Bailey-chan, you're not going to die. The water is cold but it's your fear that's making it colder than what it is. You'll find yourself in colder environments than this and if your mind freezes there, then you'll be in real difficulty. Once you're submerged, you'll find it refreshing but I want you to learn to control your mind in any given situation. I was exactly the same as you when I first visited this river. But as my Sensei taught me "*No man ever steps in the same river twice, for it's not the same river and he's not the same man*" Or should I say that every time you do this, your experience of it will change every time, but your mind will adapt to any situation once you train it. Don't think of the water, think of the warmth in your mind and the external will adapt. Water is only water, it is not the cold of it that fears you but the the possibility that it is colder than you think. Now hurry up and get in" he said pointing to it and waiting for Ronin to get in. He watched as Ronin placed a foot in and he saw shock in his eyes, but also a quiet determination that he would do it. Once he was submerged up his neck, Ronin's teeth were chattering a little but he knew he would be ok. "Now clear your mind Bailey-chan, remove the thought of cold within it. Your body and mind can survive things if you train it right. Now how are you feeling?" he asked. Ronin took a few moments and controlled his thoughts before answering. "I hate to admit it Sensei but you're right, when I first entered, it was cold of touch but once I submerged myself, then it changed. It was as if my mind turned it from cold to warm even though the water is still cold, in fact I might go for a swim" he said before submerging his head and swimming out into the slow flowing river. His Sensei chuckled as watched him, duck dive and swim around enjoying himself. "Now come Bailey-chan, or you'll really feel it soon enough" he said. Ronin swam back to the edge of the river but the biggest smile was upon his face, he stood wrapped up in a towel but the feeling of euphoria warmed his body quicker than any towel could.

"Everything good Bailey-san" a voice asked in the distance. Ronin soon switched his mind back to the present moment as he saw Sakai look at him "Yes thanks Sakai-san, just old memories of days gone by, old but good" Ronin replied.

CHAPTER THIRTY-FIVE

The first hour seemed to disappear as they ascended the trail, the air was still crisp and cool but they were starting to heat up the further up they travelled. They had stopped every thirty minutes to check their surroundings, Ronin's mind was working overtime as he questioned what lay ahead of them, the thoughts flowed through his mind as they had made their way this far. The biggest question was what would greet them at the summit, he had kept check of all the people coming down and those that would pass by when they had stopped for a rest. He knew that fear is an easy enemy to enter the mind once the thoughts flow and that can only lead to paranoia. He knew that he could hold his own and that of Sakai if need be, he was slightly worried what would happen if they did come into a contact with Yamada's men, he of course would stand his ground and fight those that came close enough to taste steel. He was looking around, taking a moment to appreciate his surroundings. He knew that if this was under any other circumstances then he could have truly enjoyed the views and take them in. He decided that if he got through this then he would return. He looked over to Sakai was taking a quick drink of water, their eyes met for only a second but for some reason Ronin saw something that he had seen before in others. It was the look of fear, Sakai diverted his eyes quickly and smiled. "How much longer do you think it will take Bailey-san?" he asked.

Ronin put all thoughts to one side and answered "We're looking at another hour Sakai-san, I've seen nothing yet that would indicate that Yamada's men are close by, but that doesn't mean that they are not here, especially if they have taken another path or trail. We've done everything we can so our movements haven't been compromised. No one knew that we would be here and we've done everything to not leave a trail. I'm not even sure if Hanzō's blade will even be upon the summit but we've got to at least attempt to check this out, we owe too many people that to not even try" He had said that last part with some emphasis to try and see if Sakai reacted to it. If their movement had been compromised then something would give it away. Sakai simply smiled and nodded "Yes Bailey-san, you're right. Let's get this done, shall we continue?" He replied.

They both took a moment to adjust their straps on their packs and set off again up the trail. The trail was beginning to ascend more steeply in places but nothing that would test them yet. It would be a slow and steady climb but worthwhile to reach the summit. The views surrounding the mountain were breathtaking and if it had been under any other circumstances then both of them would have been photographing their adventure, but this was under a very difficult situation and no time for that kind of leisure was possible.

As they were coming up to the last half mile, they slowed their pace as the summit was really starting to come ever closer and they didn't want to make it too obvious they were keen to get to their final check point. As they scanned their surroundings they saw a few clusters of people around the summit and decided to take it easy and act like the tourists they had pretended to be.

"Right Sakai-san, I think we need to make sure we're looking at the right location. According to the drone footage and intel we have, the location of the cavern is situated about two hundred metres to our left, as you can see by the central crater. If we take it easy then we can make it there and rest up close to it so we're not making any obvious movements. I'm still unsure about those clusters of people over there" Ronin said as he nodded in the direction of a cluster of about five or six people as he didn't want to use his hands as that was too obvious. They could see a small group of people, they had to make a decision of waiting or to approach.

"I think it may be wise to keep moving Sakai-san as we can't stay here or it will start to look suspicious. Let's take it slow and steady and then see if we can make a pass as we can make a judgement call, what say you Sakai-san?" Ronin asked. Sakai nodded and simply answered "Yes, you're right"

Ronin in that moment was unsure of Sakai's re-action as he thought maybe he was just being cautious but his instincts were flaring. They set off and started to close in on the cluster of people standing next to the outcrop of rocks. As they got closer, Ronin felt something wasn't right. "Slow down Sakai-san, this doesn't feel right" Ronin whispered just as one of the group reacted by rais-ing a pistol and firing off a round. The crack and thud exploded in their ears as they dropped to the ground and scrambled to the nearest outcrop of rocks to protect themselves.

The air buzzed with conflict as one of the group shouted, even though they were less than fifty metres away the words pierced Ronin's heart "Sakai-san, we told you if you carried on then we wouldn't back down. This doesn't belong to you, the people of Japan or anyone else except Yamada-san. He has claimed rights for it and nothing can stop him from claiming the rest, so your journey ends here old man" Ronin felt as though he had been sucker punched, he struggled to breath for a moment or two. Sakai betrayed him, he couldn't believe it. Out of all the people in the word, he thought he would be the last person to do so.

He looked at Sakai and just wanted to say "Why?" But he knew that this was the end of the road, they would never get close enough to get the blade. He would have to admit defeat right at the finish line. He took a deep breath and found the strength to admit that it was time to leave. Some fights are not worth the outcome. He wanted to just get up and walk away from it all but he knew he couldn't leave Sakai-san there either. Sakai sat with his head down, he looked finished, a broken man. Ronin made his choice in that moment. He took one last breath and put his hand upon Sakai's shoulder and simply said "Let's get out of here, this victory isn't ours but it isn't our last"

Sakai looked up at Ronin, the pain in his eyes said it all and yet he couldn't find it within himself to speak. He simply nodded and followed Ronin away from the outcrop. The cold air seemed to bite into him a little deeper and yet he knew that there was nothing he could say that would change anything.

CHAPTER THIRTY-SIX

The world is a dark and dangerous life without the fire of of dragons to light the way, but when the light fades a little more, the night is closer than you'll find. Anger and fear are dangerous feelings that will cloud your emotions and vision. They hold no purpose other than destruction of the senses that will make you create reckless actions and that's something that Ronin knew all too well. There was many times within his life where he had seen emotions control someone's actions that have betrayed them, leading to poor outcomes. He knew that it was all too easy to rely on anger and aggression to release the pent up emotions when unchangeable situations arise, and this was one of them. There was absolutely nothing he could change but he knew that all he could do was control his emotions and let go of what was uncontrollable. At first, he was confused and bordering on anger but he knew that wasn't the answer. For Sakai to betray him like that was unbelievable but it wasn't done out of anger but more like desperation or something far more dangerous like a checkmate situation. Ronin knew that it wasn't just them that was at risk but Sakai had a family he had to protect. Ronin knew that all he had was Emiko, a sister he thought he had lost a long time ago. He knew very well of betrayal, but this definitely seemed like a desperate situation rather than anger.

They had spoken little words between them on their descent and even the odd glances at Sakai said it all. He was a broken man and Ronin knew that no words would change that. He had to just deal with the hand he had been dealt. The odds had been stacked against them from the start and he was more bewildered and confused that he hadn't seen the cracks before they happened. What burned more was that Sakai could had said something but then again it would look more like an excuse he was using to not go ahead with the climb. He had a thousand questions he wanted to ask him but for now, that had to be left until he had confronted his own emotions when dealing with this situation. They had made it back to their rendezvous point at the base of the mountain and Ronin made as small talk as possible so not to make it worse "We need time to reassess the situation Sakai-san, once we understand what's happened, only then can we decide the next move we take. Let's give it a few days and then regroup and discuss, sound good?" He asked. Sakai could not fully look Ronin in the eye. He acted as though he was a naughty child that had been caught out, his eyes more down than up, he simply replied "Yes Bailey-san, that sounds good, I'll be seeing you"

With that they had gone their separate ways and both of them knew that the path ahead was a little darker than they had both walked before. If Yamada's men had seized the blade, if it had been there all this time, then there was nothing they could do about that. Ronin felt that he would like to know if the blade had been there all this time, more out of curiosity rather than actual facts as it would at least cleared up a mystery. Once he knew that, it would at least help him make decisions on the next move. The good part was that he knew that Yamada could do nothing else without the Tsuba and Tsuka which they both held. At least the odds were in their favour as without those two parts, there was nothing that Yamada could do or in fact prove that it was the the blade of Hanzō, it was worthless without the other parts. What could he do without the remaining parts? That brought a sense of satisfaction to Ronin. He knew that to secure his knowledge that Yamada had been successful in his find, that chatter between different fractions and organisations would soon appear on the net and he would be able to make a decision based on this. It might take a few weeks but everything comes to the man who is patient and patience was something that Ronin was good at.

Thinking about that brought him back to a childhood memory, he had been asked to wait by the side of a pond with a simple bamboo stem and line, which was attached some bait on which he was hoping would attract the one fish that lurked within its depths. He was also told that he couldn't move until the fish had been caught. That sounded like an impossible task as no one had actually caught the fish ever. They had seen its trail left in the water and bubbles appear, even once some-one had claimed to have seen it, apparently it was quite a size but that could just be fisherman's tales. Ronin had sat there through day and night, wet, cold, windswept, warm and mild nights and even after a couple of days had passed, it seemed more like the fish was playing with him. At first he was eager and hadn't slept or really moved position. But slowly, tiredness crept in and he could feel himself dropping off to sleep, which he couldn't happen. He splashed his face with cold water and done a few meditation exercises to ease his breathing. On the third day, he was ready to quit. He had enough of waiting and knew that he would rather quit with the knowledge that he tried and failed rather than not try. But then, sitting absolutely still on that edge of the pond, almost Buddha like, he felt the tug of the line dangling in the water, a light one at first that was barely noticeable. It must of been the fish nibbling at the bait and then it happened. What felt as though he was being pulled forward, almost into the pond, which he had to use all his strength through tiredness to act against. He struggled against the power of the fish as it battled against him, but slowly Ronin had began to wear down its strength until he saw the fish almost floating on the surface, making small movements. He had at last given up the fight and given into defeat. The euphoria that spread through Ronin was second to none and that he knew that patience was indeed a virtue and that all the discomfort that he had experienced was worth the end result.

And then it dawned on him, this was exactly what he would do to Yamada, he would be patient but wear him down until defeat. He knew that he had the patience to wait, but what intrigued him more was the method in which he would wear him down. He had formulated a few ideas in his mind but he knew that he would have to test them out first. Next was to confront the next task that wouldn't be easy. It had been a few days since he had seen Sakai and he knew that he would have to face him soon enough. So he decided that now was no better time to make that call.

CHAPTER THIRTY-SEVEN

The path that Ronin had chosen for this next stage of the plan was something of a challenge that even he had not thought that he could possibly even pull off, but he knew that everything rested on success. Failure wasn't an option in his mind, as he connected onto his laptop, it seemed that he had been running on autopilot for the last few days. When Sakai appeared on the screen, he looked as though he had aged a few years since the last time he had seen him. A burden seemed to rest upon his shoulders but it was something that neither of them could concentrate on, the only thing that mattered was the task ahead. They knew they could not worry about emotions right now and even though the events of the last week was something that needed to be discussed, it wasn't the main focal point of the conversation. As Ronin looked into Sakai's eyes, he saw a dark shadow within them. He still couldn't understand why he had done what he had done in one way but in another he could. He was simply protecting his family. Yamada was too good at manipulating people and using people against each other. Ronin put the events to one side, all that mattered was what they were going to do next.

"Sakai-san, I hope you are well?" Ronin asked as he looked upon a man who sat with the weight of the world upon his shoulders. Sakai looked a little distant at first but then refocused on the conversation. "Very well Bailey-san and yourself? So what's next?" He replied. Ronin had spent a great deal of time going through every scenario of what could happen but trying not to focus on a singular point of it all. He took a moment and replied "Yes, Sakai-san, good to hear and I'm good thank you. Now let's get down to what this is about shall we? The good news is that we still have the two pieces of Hanzō's sword that Yamada needs to make it complete, without those pieces, the blade means nothing. It is simply a piece of metal, but that is even if he possesses it. Even now after speaking to several contacts, it seems that there still is no actual confirmation of Yamada having it, so it could well be that he is playing a game of bluff. Those men on the mountain could have hit a dry hole and found nothing, as all the research we had carried out never confirmed that the blade was there. I have looked over the map several times and still it is not clear of the actual location. Mount Fuji was just a very good point of reference. Even if Yamada is in possession of it, it is quite useless without the other pieces that we hold. So we're still one step ahead of him. I have gone back over every piece of intel we possess and even the best of it is still sketchy. All we actually know is that Hanzō himself lived within the region and he had several locations of importance. We know that to-wards the end of his life he built a buddhist temple and became a monk. He then changed his name to 'Sainen' We know the Sainen-Ji temple still operates today and is not far from Akasaka and Shinjuku. His grave is in the same temple. Most of what's written is a lot of hearsay and as there's several versions. We know the general pieces about him. But what if the map is simply a rouse to send people in various directions away from the real source"

Both men took a moment to think about what was said. Ronin knew that his working theory on one aspect was thin at the best of times. With so many rumours and no actual proof, it would be difficult to attain real intel. But the one that he had covered and gone over several times was his best option. He looked back at Sakai, not before taking a deep breath and slowly exhaling.

"Here is one theory that's thin at the best of times Sakai-san, I know it may not have been one that we've covered as we've been so focused on the map. But what if the blade has never left Hanzō's side all this time, what if it's actually still with him? Now we could spend the next thousand years searching every possibilities and they would still turn up as only as rumours and hearsay. I suggest we focus back on Hanzō's grave at Sainen-Ji temple. We have the equipment to carry out the search and it seems that we are the only ones to hold the map itself. Now how about we let go of it?" He explained. Sakai looked a little stunned and in misbelief. He composed himself before answering "But what you're suggesting is that we hand over our only possible source of intel to the enemy? Even if we made copies then we would lose all advantage of where we're at. Yamada knew of our movements through tracking me but now he has lost that advantage. If we give him this, yes it will take him time to decipher it. Even though he has some of the best professionals in the business working on this, some of which I have consulted with on other projects. But he still has no actual reliable information at hand"

Ronin knew the plan was risky but it was their only advantage they had now and it was worth playing. He knew if they could pull this off, then they could at least buy some time and it would give them some element of surprise. He decided that this was the best option and they should act on it. He composed himself and looked back at Sakai. "I understand that this is the one advantage we have right now, even if we wait to hear if Yamada has the blade, we are still no further forward Sakai-san. But I've also realised that we also have an advantage, only we have seen the original map and know what it looks like. I know one person I can trust that could alter the map to select a few places and locations to keep Yamada busy whilst we complete our study of Sainen-Ji. Let them search in one place whilst we go in another direction. Who knows, maybe the blade was never to be found. Maybe the Tsuba and Tsuka are those of one of his favourite swords and that they are nothing special and handed them onto another. We only know of his spear and that location is known. But if you were him, would you allow your weapons far away from your final resting place?"

Sakai was taken back a bit but after a moment or two, he started to see the logic in Ronin's plan. But as they had nothing to lose, it was their best chance of possibly gaining that advantage.

CHAPTER THIRTY-EIGHT

The morning light was just starting to appear upon the horizon as Ronin exhaled his last breath of a cycle that he had been completing. Meditation to him was something that he had found to be the one place that he could find a modicum of peace, it relieved him of the chaos that filled the world in which he found himself entering on a daily basis. Breath work was something that he had began longer than he could remember but it was the one constant that remained within his life that brought that peace he longed. It allowed him to remove any negative energy that he absorbed and a place in which cycled any unwanted thoughts which he could filter. He also spent around twenty minutes of strength and conditioning exercises which kept his body supple and strong. Stretching his body from top to toe. To some, these yoga exercises was something that was difficult but to Ronin, it was exercise that kept his body flexible and helped against injuries. It seemed that he was constantly fighting against, the wear and tear that his body had endured over the many years. This set of exercises was combined with sword work, the various Katas that he completed sharpened his mind as well as his body. All various movements turned into muscle memory as he pirouetted and moved swiftly, every cut, every slash, block, jab was timed to perfection until he had completed every set of exercises. Every session that he completed was always followed by cold water therapy. Submerging himself within the water cleansed not only his mind but also his body, it refreshed him for another day, allowing him to feel alive at his maximum strength, repairing his weary body beaten and honed like a blade upon the Swordsmith's anvil.

He went through the plan again that he had devised, breaking it into several sections. The first part was underway and he was pleased that it had gone smoothly so far. Allowing the map to be altered with additional content allowed confusion to enter the minds of his enemy without them ever realising. Deception and theatricality was key to strategy, it allowed for the enemy to be tricked into making costly mistakes allowing time to be taken on other ventures. The map then being passed along through several sources into the hands of Yamada himself. According to these sources, he seemed to be in total joy of receiving them, believing that he had won the battle before it had barely began. Ronin knew that this additional time allowed him and Sakai to carry out their surveying work at Sainen-Ji temple, they would use the guise of workers being employed by a historical organisation that was mapping the temple for important information collecting purposes to allow them to understand the layout of it but also the construction of it. The survey would give them great depth and knowledge of its layout both surface and subsurface, 3D imaging that penetrated the earth using the latest technology allowed them to see what was underneath the earth. Finally, they would be able to see what was around and under Hanzō's grave. They would also be able to use X-ray technology that gave them a perspective of any hidden objects that lay there. Once this surveying had been completed, it would give them a true understanding of what was actually there and would assist them being able to adjust the plan accordingly.

They had a licence for three days to carry out the survey. That was more than enough time to collate the data and for it to be analysed. Ronin knew that once the results of the survey were in, then he could make the needed changes that would allow them to carry out the next part. If he was right about Hanzō's grave, then he would gain an advantage that Yamada would know nothing of. Even if he was suspicious of the surveying work at the temple, they had gone through several organisations which held official government accreditation which Sakai had used before. Everything was done at a level in which several layers had been added and they knew that Yamada would be more concentrating on the map itself.

Whilst the surveying was carried out, that all's allowed both Ronin and Sakai to discuss what was next. They both knew that even if they were successful in their findings, they weren't even sure what would happen when they had all the pieces of this puzzle. They both agreed that Yamada's greed would take over and he would do whatever it took to get it. Everything they did was for the people and to give back to them. Individuals like Yamada only believed in personal greed and ego. Everything else was expendable. They knew that the next couple of days would be crucial to the plan and whatever happened next would change everything. After their last online meeting, they both agreed that they would meet up in a secure location to finalise the next steps.

CHAPTER THIRTY-NINE

The last few days had been a flurry of activity and both Ronin and Sakai had spent it deciding what was to happen next. They both knew that the plan had started to fall into place as the reports coming back were showing that the plan was working well. Yamada had indeed fallen for the fake map and sent out people to investigate the new leads. This had allowed a gap to be created so they could send in surveyors to Sainen-Ji to study the temple and it's grounds. For what reports they had received, the area around Hanzō's grave were starting to show some good results.

They both stood their over a large table with laptops and a few large pieces of paper with technical drawings and illustrations. What was shown on them hadn't been seen ever and they knew that they were the first to ever see this kind of imaginary. They had spent the last few hours looking through the 3D illustrations on the large screen. Ronin was standing closer to the screen looking at all the points and although he wasn't technically trained he could see what they wanted to know. He pointed out a couple of areas detailed. "As you can see here and here Sakai-san, there's several anomalies in and around Hanzō's grave area, especially underneath it. That to me looks like a shaft leading off and it's big enough to be a tunnel system. Now if we pull up this data from this temple website, we can see that the temple is known as Senshozan Annyo-in Sainen-ji and it was founded by the honorable Hanzō Masanari Hattori, a legendary ninja, to commemorate honorable Nobuyasu Matsudaira, who as we know was Tokugawa Ieyasu's eldest son. Now with historical accounts, they detail that In Tensho 18th, which is in the year 1590, Ieyasu entered Edo, he built Edo Castle and established the principal base. Hanzō Masanori had also entered Edo following Ieyasu, but he shaved his hair to enter the Buddhist priesthood to pray for the soul of Nobuyasu and changed his name to 'Sainen'. He then built a hut in Kojimachi Shimizudani which is near the Hotel New Otani and Shimizudani Park) He buried the hair of Nobuyasu which he had embraced since he left Enshu, and prayed for Nobuyasu day after day. Now it was also recorded that in Bunroku 2 which is 1593, Hanzō had received 300 ryo. 1 ryo is approximately equivalent to 1,000 United States Dollars from Ieyasu and was ordered to use the money to build a temple to pray for the soul of Nobuyasu, the loyal people to the Tokugawa family as well as for the enemies who were killed in the various battles.

However it also states that he could not fulfill the order to build a temple and passed away at the age of 55 on November 14, Bunraku 4 which is 1595. Hanzō's Buddhist name is '専称院殿(Senshoinden) 安譽(Anyo) 西念 (Sainen) 大禅定門 (Daizenjomon) Thereafter, a temple was built where the hut was, and the temple's name including prefixes was after his Buddhist name, 専称山(Sensho-san) 安養院(Anyo-in) 西念寺(Sainen-ji).

In Kanei 11, which is 1634, in order to establish the outer moat accompanying the extension of the Edo Castle outer passages, the shogunate government decided temples should be collectively located outside the moat and this temple was also moved to its present place.

Unfortunately though, in May, Showa 20 which is 1945, all buildings were destroyed in the war, and the main hall was rebuilt at the end of November, Showa 36 which is 1961. After that, with cooperation from the congregation and related people, they built the priest quarters, the reception hall, and other buildings. Now what's not being shown is that like a lot of historical buildings, they are built upon the ruins of others and no where is it listed that these tunnels exist. They seem to run to the main building, that's it's possible entrance point Sakai-san. What's your thoughts?" Ronin asked as he turned and looked at Sakai.

Sakai had taken a moment to take in all that he was looking at the screen before answering, he exhaled and looked at Ronin "Yes, you are absolutely correct Bailey-san, these tunnels are not documented anywhere that we've seen and not even on anything official, so even Yamada wouldn't know if it. I feel that this time, an element of luck is on our side. If we can gain access to the internal of the main temple then we could possibly find the main entrance to it. If we are quick enough, then we can explore this tunnel and see what's actually there and back out before Yamada ever knew that we had discovered this. Hopefully the map will keep him busy allowing us this time to try and get one step forward" Sakai replied.

Ronin nodded and answered "Right, we will collect all our equipment needed and make one final check before we head over to the temple. Let's hope that this time our efforts are not thwarted by Yamada. We have done everything we can to not get this far to fail. Let's say that we regroup here tomorrow and head over to the temple to start our investigation, what say you Sakai-san?"

"Sounds like a plan to me Bailey-san, let's truly hope that the gods are on our side this time"

CHAPTER FORTY

"**Y**ou must find them for they are in grave danger and you need to protect them" said the voice. They weren't even sure who this was but they knew that it was the truth spoken as they had been spending last week searching for them and it was if they had become ghosts. They knew the mission was going to be one of the most important of their life. Ronin and Sakai had become persons of interest in the Yamada circle and that was never a good thing. If they were on that watch list then they had better watch their backs. They had heard rumours in the last week of Yamada receiving a map that led to the lost blade of Hanzō, but if it even existed they weren't even sure. The message was definitely a warning and even when they replayed it, they knew that it was time to dig a little deeper to find them. What they had done at the mountain was only the beginning and they knew that there was more to come. They knew Yamada and what he was capable of, especially as their late father had some business dealings with and they ended badly. Yamada was ruthless, especially in their execution of anyone who got in his way. They decided that it was definitely time to act and to find them. For a brother they had never been aware of, they were in a state of shock at first. When the truth was revealed and that Tanaka had adopted a few children such as Ronin and Emiko, making them family. Being the only true daughter of Tanaka was hard to live with these days. All his physical assets had been divided when he died, even though they had received a smaller percentage than expected. They made a choice that they would do good with them like set up a few children's charities to help orphans and others, to give them the life they deserve. They had to get to work in tracking them down and fast before Yamada got hold of them, for they had received warnings that Yamada himself had put a bounty on their heads and anyone who captured them would receive a generous undisclosed amount. The whole of Tokyo was full of individuals who thrived in this kind of sport and both Ronin and Sakai would be unaware of this bounty, making anywhere they actually travelled a risk. They decided to move fast and track both of them down with any intel they had before any harm fell upon them.

"Are you completely sure you understand the plan Sakai-san" asked Ronin as he stood next to a table with a map on it. Several pointers had been situated on it. Sakai nodded and agreed. Ronin had gone over the plan several times to make sure it as risk free as possible but no plan ever survived first contact. To him, he just had to roll with it and deal with any issues as they came across them. He had kept it as simple as possible, to minimise risk, he had split their routes between them. They would leave the safe house at different times in different vehicles and take different routes. That way it would reduce the ability for anyone tracking them to surprise them. They had stay as low key as possible as Ronin knew what was at stakes. He knew very well that since what had happened on Mount Fuji that Sakai had been compromised, but that was understandable as Yamada was ruthless and often targeted a persons family to throw threats, which were not to be taken lightly. Both vehicles were packed with kit, they did contain firearms, but only if needed and driven by securely sourced close protection drivers who could react quickly to any situation. Ronin knew that this had to be done properly, they had been able to gain access to Sainen-Ji for a few hours whilst it was closed to the general public, that would minimise any risk as well. The last feedback that Ronin was given was that Yamada had taken the map hook, line and sinker. He had sent out small teams to investigate the leads, but Ronin knew that he would not be forgetting either himself or Sakai. Knowing the way that Yamada worked and his modus operandi, he would have people out searching for both of them. That meant that they would have to move fast and work quickly. Of there was any truth in finding the lost blade of Hanzō then they would need to carry out their search under the upmost secrecy as possible.

The vehicles were checked for the last time, Ronin was fairly confident that they would succeed in making a covert infil of the temple but he knew that time was against them, they had to work quickly. "You all good Sakai-san?" Ronin asked over the secure network. "Yes, all good thanks, I will wait for your next check in Bailey-san. If this all goes to plan then we should be able to be in and out of the temple in minimum time without any knowledge of us being there, speak soon" Sakai replied. As he sat there waiting for departure, he knew the odds they were up against. The warning from Yamada had not left him. Even though he knew what he had done to Ronin would not be forgotten lightly, he only hoped that Ronin would understand that he had to protect his family at all costs against the likes of Yamada. Especially after his own dealings with his father and what had happened. Men like Tanaka and Yamada were not people who ever gave second chances and Sakai knew that they were very much driving straight into that second chance as though it were a roadblock. "Sakai, you're good to go, see you on location soon, over and Godspeed" was all that played through the net as Sakai's vehicle started and pulled out of the bay into the night. What awaited them, only the shadows knew.

CHAPTER FORTY-ONE

"We must get this done now and quickly, do you understand? We mustn't allow the blade to be discovered by them or they will potentially unlock the power it holds" said the voice emulating from the screen. They took a moment to think about what had been said and decided to reply "Yes, I'm perfectly aware of what's at stake and what Yamada's intentions are. I know he wants this power for himself and we have the maps in our possession. It won't take long and we shall have it. We've sent enough men to track it down and it shall only be a few days and then he shall have it back. I know what happened on Mount Fuji wasn't what Yamada wanted and yet we have the situation fully under control. We have done everything we can especially as Sakai knows what is at stake. Like I've mentioned, give me a few days and it shall be back in the hands of the rightful owner" they replied as the looked at the screen. The fuzzy image replied "Good, and now for our next part, for we know Ronin and Sakai intend to visit Sainen-Ji soon to use any kind of information there, but believe me that's not going to happen. We've been tracking them for the last few days and know what is going to happen next. Our reach is far longer then they are even aware of. Now let's get this done, I don't want to let Yamada down again or even someone like myself is not untouched by Yamada's wrath" They explained as the screen faded to black leaving them pondering what to do next. They knew that what was happening and what was needed to happen was inescapable. The wrestled between conscious and reality. Yamada's reach was truly far and yet even from that time on the ship when revenge was flowing through their veins. Even dragon mountain was something that they never thought would happen as they had not expected help from high places. If that happens again, they had not only Ronin and Sakai to eliminate but also a third party that was unknown to them. The stakes we're getting high and they knew that time was against him, he had to make a decision and even if Yamada's men were successful and retrieved the blade, they also had a task ahead to prevent, especially Ronin from getting anywhere near it. He knew of his true capabilities, he had witnessed it with his own eyes. Now it was time to get to work.

"Check, check, radio check Sakai-san, can you hear me loud and clear" Ronin asked as he pressed the button on his throat mic. "Loud and clear Bailey-san" replied Sakai. "Good, let's get this done. Wit the intel we have on Sainen-Ji, we know that there is a potential entrance to the underground tunnel system that runs to Hanzō's grave in the main building. We need to get inside and into it before anyone else knows. This is going to be difficult at the best of times. I'm hoping that the fake maps that were distributed are enough to keep Yamada's men busy until we get in and out and hopefully we'll have the blade. Right, let's stay off the airwaves until we reach the temple. We'll be travelling in two convoys and those two routes have been travelled and tested, no major diversions and yet we have alternative routes if needed. If and I truly mean if anything does go wrong, especially as we've been getting some kind of transmissions that Yamada may have some indications of our actions, then we fall onto plan B. It's the last case scenario, but it'll work, you understand Sakai-san" Ronin asked as he sat back in the passenger seat of the truck. "Perfectly clear and understood" Sakai replied. "Good, let's head out and Godspeed" Ronin said as they drove out of the garage. Only faith can get you so far and blind luck takes over. Ronin knew the stakes of this game of cat and mouse. He had played it once before with his own father and had won, but he knew that it wouldn't always be that way.

Everything about this wasn't about one person, it was far bigger than that. It was about an entire nation. If they could pull this off, then a piece of history could be complete and finally laid to rest. Even if that meant the sacrifice of himself to achieve the end goal, then he was willing to do this. He knew that time was always against him with this one and only the ticking hands could determine it's outcome.

As he laid back travelling through the streets, dusk was just settling and yet the thrive of activity was just starting to settle. The route they had set on was fairly standard and they had spent time travelling it a couple of times. From the various transmissions, the temple was still secure and no unusual activity so far but that could change. As they were travelling in identical trucks, both with blackened windows, then Yamada would need to make a choice of which vehicle to strike as he would be the main target as Yamada knew that Sakai was just a passenger in this chapter and that he was no threat to him. Ronin was still a still a little wary of how Sakai would react, especially after the Mount Fuji incident, which he knew wasn't his fault. But he must put all these thoughts to one side and concentrate on what's ahead rather than was behind. All that mattered was the mission and retrieving the blade. He was certain that this was it, all he needed to do was keep focused on the end goal. They came up to a junction and started to turn off onto the road they needed when a frantic voice came through Ronin's throat mic "They're onto us Bailey-san, we're going to have to fall onto plan B, I'm sorry" And with that, Ronin tightened his fists as the fear of not being able to do anything was gripping his body. He knew that this was the last place he wanted to be, torn between going after Sakai and getting to the temple. But he knew what was needed to be done and he knew that Sakai would understand.

CHAPTER FORTY-TWO

"On the next corner, stop the truck and I'll get out there" Ronin said. The driver nodded in understanding. Ronin knew that if Plan B was going to work, then he would need to make changes that levelled the playing field. The only way he could do that was on his own terms. As they came to the corner of the next street, he had his hand on this kit and ready to get out. They were fast approaching the corner and in his mind, Ronin had already prepared his exit from the vehicle and onto the streets. Three, two, one and the vehicle came to an abrupt halt and within seconds Ronin had exited the vehicle. He had swung his kit onto his back and threw his hood up and over his head. He was moving fast, the streets darkened as the night crept in. He kept his breathing calm and collected as he quickly made his way through the streets, he kept a good pace as he made his way towards the temple. He knew that his only hope lay in doing what he was good at and that was hiding in plain sight, slipping between the evening crowds within the slightly crowded streets.

As he made his way towards the temple, he kept scanning the crowds, constantly on the look for anyone who resembled Yamada's men but he knew that they would be on the lookout for him. As he approached the temple entrance, he saw a couple of people that just didn't seem right to him. He swerved past a couple of people and headed for the main gates. There was a group of people heading into the parking area, quite possibly towards the main temple. Just as he merged within this crowd, he noticed a couple of men standing there and knew that they would be on the lookout for him. He kept perfectly calm as he stayed to the left of the crowd using them to cover his movements. Just as they levelled with the entrance he was able to swerve to his far left and in with a couple of others without any questions. He knew that this was the only way he would have accessed the temple without detection. It was close though as he kept scanning the area in front of him. He knew that he had been fortunate to have got this far but he knew that there would be others.

As he approached the main entrance of the temple he had to drop back his pace as he saw a couple of men standing by the doorway. He couldn't slow down his approach, neither could he make it obvious that he was there. So he did what seemed obvious to him. He had already slipped a hand into one of his pockets and pulled out a small thin tube with a ring pull on the top. He had slipped a finger through the ring and timed his approach well as he removed it and began to count. On the count of three he threw the tube hard to his right and a couple of seconds later chaos erupted as the flash bang went off. It was like a series of fire crackers had been lit, except the noise and light it created was deafening and blinding as people screamed and threw their hands up to their ears and eyes. Ronin used his hood to shield his eyes the best he could, his ears were already protected with the noise cancelling ear piece he was wearing to communicate with Sakai. He made his way quickly through the doors and then he saw it, Hanzō's spear, or otherwise known as "Oni Hanzo" and has been worshiped by Ieyasu Tokugawa for numerous military achievements. It was still an impressive weapon even though the tip had been broken off by an earthquake during the Ansei era and the handle had been burnt by the air raids of World War II. It was indeed long, measuring at about 258 cm, the thickness is about 5 cm, and the weight is about 7.5 kg. It has been registered as a cultural property of Shinjuku Ward.

Ronin knew that time was against him after releasing the flash bang as he knew that the police would have been notified and making their way. He had less than ten minutes. But he was confident after spending hours going through the plan multiple times and going through every eventuality. He had even memorised the steps from the entrance doors to the area in which the entrance to the tunnel system was located. He knew from imagery and also first hand knowledge that the tunnel entrance was hidden in what was classed as a cupboard to the right of the main shrine. It was a tight fit but one he knew he could get in. He couldn't believe that no one knew of its existence. As he pulled the door open, he squatted and withdrew a blade before running it under the edge of the flooring, which he then lifted revealing what looked like flooring but what was actually a trapdoor. He slid the original panel to one side and then ran his fingers over the panel and found what he was looking for, a small ring which he slid the blade in and lifted. Once it was fully uncovered he slid a finger into it and pulled up. It took a couple of hard pulls and it loosened. As he lifted, he felt cold air coming from beneath. He pulled up until he could rest it up against a wall.

This was it, now it never as he pulled out a head torch from one of his pockets and slipped off his hood before fitting it on his head. He switched it on and shone the light beneath him which revealed a tunnel. He could see the bottom of the shaft, which was not that deep but it was deep enough for him to move through. He dropped his legs over the edge and knew that he would have to reposition the panel to hide his movements. He judged it to be at least just over one and a half metres deep, he thought himself lucky as he was nearly six foot. That allowed him to reach the panel and drop it back down on him. As he dropped into the shaft he made sure he slid the door behind him and then lifted the panel up and down to cover him in darkness. The only light was what was shining in front of him from his head torch. He had to bend down as he made his way through the tunnel running his hand against the rough hewed wall. He could feel the gouge marks made many generations ago. He kept his mind clear as he had no thoughts of doubt of what was ahead, the blade would either be here or it wasn't. He found the tunnel slowly begin to slope down as though he was going deeper until it levelled out again after a couple of metres. He had put all thoughts of events happening above as he knew that Yamada's men would have scattered once the police were there. They had intentionally already set that up for them to arrive within minutes of Ronin releasing the flash bang. As he crawled through, he was confident that this was going to be a success. He shone the light ahead and there it was, he couldn't believe it. He was moving his head torch slowly as he approached the shrine that had been carved into the walls, floors and ceiling of this purpose built chamber, directly beneath the tomb of Hattori Hanzō himself.

CHAPTER FORTY-THREE

Ronin could feel the raw power emulating from the shrine in front of him. It was as if there was a kind of dark magic, electrifying from it, crackling in the atmosphere. As he stepped forward he found himself modulating his breathing, bringing him back to a place which he was comfortable within. He reached out and placed his hand upon the blade that was laying on a stand atop a rock placement that had been carved out of the ground in which he stood. As his fingers touched it, it was as if a power was flowing through him. He had never felt anything like it before. He thought that maybe it was just him but thoughts that came flowing through him, it was almost like having an out of body experience but he was stood perfectly still. Memories of his childhood rushed through him and then in that very moment he knew that it was his time. Whatever happened next, he knew that it would never be the same again. Then he realised, this was exactly why Yamada wanted this power, he craved it.

He slipped his hand around the cold piece of metal

that served as a placement area for both the Tsuba and Tsuka which he carried with him. He felt a slow pulsating feeling and then realised it was his own heart beating deeply within. He let go and moved his hand down to the satchel he carried with him, within lay the Tsuba and Tsuka, which he removed and lay them next to the blade. He felt a weird connection between all three as he picked up the blade in one hand and the Tsuba in the other. He fitted it, sliding it into place. Next to go was the Tsuka which slid on and then he reached within the satchel. He pulled out a string draw bag which he had been carrying all this time, he had found them within the casket within dragon mountain but said nothing. These were the metal pins that secured the Tsuka to the blade. And then it was complete, it was done.

He stood holding after all these years the very blade that Hanzō had held within his very hands and at that moment, his life had made sense. This was what it all meant. He was the one person who was supposed to discover it. But now what to do with it, Ronin wasn't sure as if he made contact with Sakai and told him. Would that only lead to Yamada pursuing it? He let out a deep exhale and breath and decided he would deal with that as it came. But first he would get out of here and then make sure that Sakai was safe. Firstly he would need to give thanks to Hanzō in the only way he knew. He placed the complete sword back upon the hewn stand and stepped back and bowed before he kneeled upon the floor. He would perform the very ceremony that he did before he trained. The very ceremony he had had performed with his Sensei all those years ago. He could see it now within his minds eye. His Sensei kneeled in front of him with his hands both closed above his head closed in a prayer posture slowly rubbing them together, this movement was then closely followed by himself who patiently waited for the next part. *"Shikin Haramitsu Daikomyo"* the Sensei spoke with clarity and purpose when speaking these words, which was then followed by himself.

As he had learned many years ago, the translation of them are somewhat of a mixed understanding with many, but roughly it translated as - Shikin - A greeting, sensation of harmony, perceived by the heart. Harimitsu - Wisdom from courage and effort fosters sincerity, loyalty and faithfulness. Daikomyo - Bring respect and reliance, illumination from the inside to the outside. Taken together, Every encounter is sacred and could present the one potential key to the perfection of the great universal enlightenment we seek. The Sensei then made two sudden claps which once again he repeated after him. The Sensei then bowed towards the floor, Ronin then matched his timing. Once again the Sensei raised his closed palms to clap only once this time. Ronin felt that the two collisions of palms made the air boom within the large dojo.

This ceremony was something that Ronin had performed hundreds of times over the years and it was second nature by now. He then stood up and bowed once more, giving thanks to Hanzō himself before picking up the sword and with a cloth sword bag he had removed from the satchel, slid the sword within. He turned around and headed back the way he came until he reached the panel that he pushed up slowly and looking over the edge. The door was still slid shut which was good and it seemed to be quiet. He lifted the panel above him and rested it behind him against the wall. He slid the sword to one side before lifting himself out of the tunnel. He then placed the panel back and then the second one before slowly sliding opening the door and scanned the area in front of him. He could see movement over by the front entrance but he was prepared to deal with that once he got there. He stepped out of the cupboard and across the floor until he reached the entrance. He watched the movements outside and listened to the muffled voices, trying to understand what was being said, but couldn't. He was about to step forward and then a lights shone upon him from a couple of positions, from either side of the temple floor and then a voice "Bailey-san, we must move quickly, Sakai-san is in danger" when they stood forward into the pale light Ronin took a massive gulp of oxygen as his eyes widened. He couldn't believe who was standing there after all this time "Kenji Tanaka, what are you doing here *brother*" Ronin said in a way that projected the last part with a emphasis, whilst regaining his composure. He knew that it was never good if Kenji was standing there.

CHAPTER FORTY-FOUR

"It's not good Bailey-san, Sakai-san's vehicle was apprehended a few blocks from here by Yamada's men. He's now on his way to a secure location to be questioned by Yamada himself and that's never good. When we first knew of the possibility that Hanzō's sword actually existed, there was a chance that Yamada would find out. There's been a lot of chatter over the last few months that Yamada was sending out his people to source possible locations of this sword. You know now of its power it holds and this is what Yamada wants. He believes that if he holds this sword then it would give him power over a lot of people, we would see destruction on a level that's not been seen in a long time. He's been going after the old families, slowly destroying them for the last few years, acquiring as much wealth as possible. He needs to be stopped, it's as simple as that. When he tried to come after what was left of the Tanaka family, that's when we decided that his rule of the criminal underground needed to be stopped. He has amassed a small fortune and has become incredibly powerful in a short time. Even the Japanese government are beginning to fear him, he isn't powerful enough to confront the Yamaguchi-gumi yet though. The old Yakuza families are the only thing stopping him from making a claim for the highest position in all of Japan. We need to stop him permanently though and you're the only person who can do it. The families have been trying for the last year to infiltrate Yamada's internal organisation but the ones who have been caught have never been seen again. I know me and you have never spoken since what happened with father, but if peace is to be achieved before a war is started that could destroy all of Japan, then we need to act now" Benji explained as he looked at Ronin.

Ronin wasn't even sure what to think at that moment, all this time he had been entirely focused on retrieving the sword and handing it back to the people of Japan. But now the whole game had changed, especially with the Yamaguchi-gumi now stepping in as they are the largest yakuza family, with about 8,200 members. This was never good and Ronin knew how this could end. This could indeed tear the whole of Japan apart and see a civil war that would not only rival the war of 1861 in America but far worse. The only action would be to work alongside Benji and to stop Yamada before it does implode. He looked at Benji and although there was a part of him that wasn't even sure what to say, he knew that it was time to act. "I agree with you Tanaka-san, you are right, our indifferences need to be put to one side if we are going to prevent Yamada from creating something none of us are going to see the end of. But I also want to see Sakai-san safe, he only found himself in this position because of me. I know that you were sent to stop me yourself and that's why I can't understand what changed for you to be here right now, to actually want to help, there's been a lot of bad blood between us, and I know that you wanted to seek vengeance upon the person who killed your father in cold blood. You were there that night, you saw what happened with your father. Even though I was adopted and I know that it tears a little piece from you for it to be said that we were 'brothers' but that's exactly what we are. All we can do is to start working together if we want to rescue Sakai-san and end this for once and for all. I know that this may well be something that I shall not return from and there's going to be a lot of blood lost, but it is what it is and that can't be changed. As I've learned over the years *'Destiny and fate are cruel masters of humanity as they fight for the soul of man, no true redemption can be found without the sacrifice of the truth. Only the darkest of days will be enlightened by the acts of those that are willing to ring the bells of their own redemption'* Now let's get to work and start to put a plan together to get Sakai-san back and end this for once and for all" Ronin said as he looked into Benji's eyes to see his true intentions but there was nothing there to say they were not anything less than honourable.

"You're right Bailey-san, there was a time that I wanted to see you suffer after what happened with father. That nearly destroyed me in my revenge. I was given intel of what you were doing and I allowed my own anger to betray my understanding of this situation. But now that all changes. I have my own team at hand that have been selected for this task, they all know the risks and fully accept this. I suggest we get ourselves to a secure location we've set up a few miles from here and then decide what the best course of action is, I know we haven't got much time and the walls are slowly closing on us" Benji replied.

Time was truly against them and Ronin knew that better than anyone else. He knew that not only had he got to rescue Sakai, but also confront Yamada himself. He knew that this was something that he was not going to come back from and he fully accepted death for what it was. He had embraced it a long time ago and he knew what his fate would hold.

CHAPTER FORTY-FIVE

T he room was quite spacious, artwork lined the walls and the ambient lighting illuminated the various workbenches and sideboards. The central table held many maps and papers that held the information that had been acquired through several sources over a period of time. Surrounding the table stood several people who were discussing various subjects in a low tone. The door on the western wall opened and in through walked Yamada himself, he entered with a powerful presence that automatically demanded respect. Those surrounding the table stopped what they were doing and turned towards him. As Yamada made his way towards the centre of the room he spoke softly "So what do we know? How far are we finding the true location of the blade?" His voice carried a soft undertone but with a presence that spilled with power.

One of the group spoke up "Yamada-san, we are very close to finalising the actual location. All of the various places we have checked have failed to have brought any significant finds. It seems that we have exhausted any possibilities of it being where we thought it was and now working on a few locations that could hold more substance to them. Now we have Sakai, this may bring some light but he is holding back I feel and we don't want to entirely break him or it will be for nothing. There are rumours that the family are doubling their efforts of preparing to counteract any offensive measures we take. Apparently, they have spoken and feel that we are slowly becoming a threat to the stability of the clans"

Yamada tightened his eyes as he focused upon the man speaking, his fist done the same in anger as he prepared to speak "They are fools, the blade is out there, lost for hundreds of years and yet who are they to think that it belongs to no one except me? I am the only one that deserves to hold its power. If it is as powerful as it has been written about, then only myself could wield such power. We know Hanzō had a significant contribution to Tokugawa Ieyasu's rise to power, helping the future Shogun bring down the Imagawa clan. This is what they fear, that I shall become more powerful than any Shogun that has lived.

As you've all seen within these documents, Hanzō's most valuable contribution came in 1582 following Oda Nobunaga's death, when he led the future Shogun Tokugawa Ieyasu to safety in Mikawa Province across Iga territory with the help of remnants from the local Iga-ryū ji-samurai clans as well as Kōga-ryū, which were the neighbouring local samurai families in the nearby Koka region. Hanzō himself was principal in serving as Leyasu's guide and commanded 300 ninja guards to ensure his lords safe passage to Mikawa. Even when Nobuyasu was accused of treason and conspiracy by Oda Nobunaga and was then ordered to commit seppuku by his father Leyasu. Hanzō was called in to act as the official second to end Nobuyasu's suffering, but he refused to take the sword on the blood of his own lord. Ieyasu valued his loyalty after hearing of Hanzo's ordeal and said, "Even a demon can shed tears" So what I am saying is that someone who had the power in his hands of life and death was given respect by the most powerful man in the land, the families will soon understand that I am uniting them all under one blade"

The room was silent for a few moments as they contemplated what was happening. Only when one of them spoke and that seemed they this was done out of fear rather than respect. "Yamada-san, when the families hear of our true plans, they will surely revolt against us and then we will have a war that I fear none of us will survive. Why not give it back to the people of Japan and then you will be seen as a great man, the man who united the land and the people, rather than something less savoury? Surely, if we found the blade then we could use it to our advantage?" There was a moment of silence as Yamada stood contemplating what had been said.

When he spoke and it was some depth, it was from a place he had never spoken before "All of you here right now have fought to be here, we have spent years building and amassing this business to be almost one that rivalled the greatest of all the families, and yet they all fear that as soon as we find the blade it will tip the scales of power into our hands and we shall use it to destroy them. When we do find that blade it will allow all of our own families to live in a peace that none of us has known. Sometimes you have to raise a fist to show your true intentions rather than bow your head to the ground. We are on the verge of discovering one of and quite possibly the greatest artefact that Japan has ever known and not one person will stop us, send out more men to search the marked locations and I want regular updates. We have enough people to cover the search areas. Now let's meet again tomorrow and we shall discuss our progress. In the meantime, put a little more pressure on Sakai to get what you can out of him. Ronin is still out there and he is not an easy man to find either. He will come for Sakai and when he does, it will be the greatest mistake he's ever made. A bigger one than ever slaying his own father and allowing myself to dominate his wealth he left behind, so at least that is something I can be thankful of. Now let's go" Yamada said as he turned to head out of the room.

The silence that fell was as cold and deathly as any man had ever known. There was a lot to play for and yet they knew that it was never going to end well either way.

CHAPTER FORTY-SIX

"So what are we looking at then" Said Ronin, standing over a set of blueprints. The room was darkened except the lights behind upon a table which an enlarged set of blueprints of Yamada's headquarters lay in detail.

One of Ronin's technical team had spent a few hours previously printing off the blueprints and fitting them together to show the entire layout of Yamada's headquarters with details of several layers. It showed all the grounds and various layers, also backed up with drone footage on two screens and a 3D model on a table. Ronin was impressed with what had been achieved over the last couple of days. He knew that time was against them, especially with Sakai being captured and knowing the ha would be interrogated to gain as much intel as possible from Yamada's men. They had been discussing all the details of the next moves they should take.

One of Ronin's technical team spoke first, "As you can see here and here" explaining the two areas on the 3D model as well as the blueprints, pointing at various points with a pointer. "This area here and here are most likely showing Yamada's areas of operations. The other areas here are where we believe that Sakai is being held. There's a couple of possible points of entrance into Yamada's compound. We know it's secured by a highly encrypted security system and patrolled by armed guards on a rota system. We had to capture as much intel as possible in a short amount of time, especially with the drone footage, not alerting Yamada of our plans but he will be wary that a rescue attempt will happen. As you can see, his headquarters is highly secure and there's a lot of security personal in and around the area. The points of entry that we've identified is protected by a series of security measures but we know that we can override them but movement into the compound will have to be quick. Time is definitely against us, especially as they will be on high alert to a rescue attempt. They will be waiting. As you can see here and here on this part" they explained pointing to the blueprint, which also showed upon the 3D model. "These are your best entry point and they are not easy to get past. This part of the wall is secured not only by laser beams running an inch around it at several points moving up, but with digital cameras moving on a swivel system to capture any movement, several motion sensors built in here and here. But we've managed to set up a bug whilst hacking into part of the system. Once you've gained entry at this point, you will have to move quick but also avoiding these roaming patrols. They are armed with the latest weaponry and night vision goggles, so they are not blind to any movements around them. You will need to move to this point here to this small area next to the ground floor to gain entrance into the main building. We did look for any entrance points underground, but believe me, it's actually easier this way. When viewing all the options, I did gain some insight from a few special forces operatives on their opinion with this type of building and how they would approach it, but short of a High Altitude Low Opening parachute infil, which isn't possible for you as you're not trained in. This is the best option available to us. We've installed a few counter measures of our own, with time relayed glitches in the system to trick it into seeing the same loop repeated, but without alerting the main server. You'll have minimum time to get past them and into the main compound and then into the building. The stakes are high and there's no backup for this Ronin" they explained.

Ronin stood for a moment or two looking over both the blueprints and 3D model. He knew that it wouldn't be easy at all, but he needed to get this done, to get Sakai back. He wouldn't leave anyone behind, especially after Emiko, that would never leave him and he vowed it would never happen again. He needed to get this done, he had been preparing his equipment whilst the tech team had been working on this intel. He knew he had an excellent team behind him and he trusted them, especially as he had handpicked them. They were the best team he had been able to assemble at a short notice. Usually, with a task, he would tap into a couple of resources to build the intel. But this time, it was different.

He knew the team was ready and didn't want to waste anymore time going over the plan. He had enough intel and knew what needed to be done. He looked up and around at the group of individuals around him. "Let's get this done, we will get Sakai back, even if he's the only one that comes back" he said. Ronin knew the stakes on this one. He had pushed his luck enough times to know that everything had its limits and he was finally reaching it. He also knew that getting back Sakai was the honourable act as he had been crucial in every way. Ronin never held anything against him for what had happened upon Mount Fuji, that was just bad luck but totally understandable, especially as Sakai has a family to protect. Ronin had Emiko, that was all. But he knew enough that he would do whatever he could to protect her.

Ronin turned and walked towards the door but stopped and turned around to look at the team, he knew what he wanted to say but it lingered a little too long with hesitation. He nodded and simply said "Let's get Sakai home to his family"

CHAPTER FORTY-SEVEN

"What do you see James? It looks like the path is clear but I need your clearance first. I don't want to move forward if there's an immediate risk in front. What's the drone feedback look like?" Ronin asked in a low voice as he pressed on his throat mic. The night sky was fairly clear as he scanned the area in front of him. He kept looking around as he waited for some kind of feedback from the control room. He was well hidden and a distance back from the perimeter wall, he knew that it would take him approximately five minutes to get onto the ground in front of the wall and that the security measures could be hacked so that he could get over the wall. That was the easy part, once he was over the wall and into the compound, he would have to make his way past a mix of roaming patrols. The view through his night vision goggles were a clear green which displayed the ground in front of him with darkened shapes. He knew that these were the latest generation of NVG's that he had sourced from his military contact and they were currently being used by some of the top tier special forces in the world.

"You're clear to proceed Ronin and the security measures have been hacked to give you a small window to operate in. The drone footage is returning as showing about four to five guards on roaming patrols, armed with M4 rifles. If you move now, you'll be able to make it over the wall and you have a few minutes to readjust once over, I'll count you down for the measures to be hacked. Three…… Two…… One….. GO" James replied.

Ronin lifted his body as he swiftly made his way forward towards the bottom of the wall. He crouched at the foot of it as he slid his hand into one of his pouches and brought out a gas powered grappling hook gun. As he aimed up towards the point in which the hook would catch, allowing him to pull himself up to the top of the wall. The gun was quiet as it fired with a slight thud and as Ronin watched the projectile fire up and release, slowing down near the top of the wall, as it engaged and the barbed hooks dug into the brick, he pulled back to test his weight, it held.

He flipped one of the switches on the gun and allowed it to start winding the cable back pulling him upwards. He kept his body close to the wall but slightly angled back. With every metre covered Ronin was cautious not to make any excess noise. As he reached the top of the wall he made sure that he would be able to get over but within the times set to avoid the next roaming patrol. He rested his body atop the wall and scanned the ground below him. He lay perfectly still as he watched a couple of guards make their way coming his way. He was like an animal crouched ready to strike as he lay there waiting for them to pass. As they did, he slid his body over and holding onto the grappling gun in one hand and the wall with the other he lowered himself down. The hook was still embedded into the wall as he pressed the wire release mechanism which wound the cable out. As he was getting to the bottom of his descent, he waited and positioned himself lower to the ground. According to the intel he had so far, the next patrol would be passing in about five minutes but he knew if he moved now, he could get between the last one that had passed and the one approaching. He turned and looked up as he pressed a button on the gun as the hooks released themselves and allowed the cable to rewind back into their housing. Every mission he had ever done relied on two important factors, one was good intel and the other was kit. He wouldn't compromise on either.

Ronin watched as he saw some movement to the right of him at a distance and knew that was the incoming patrol. That meant that he would have less than four minutes to make his way along this perimeter and to the next checkpoint near the lower building which would become his access point. He had just adjusted his pouch he had returned his grappling gun into and made sure it was secure.

He quickly made his way along the perimeter, at least he knew that the security measures had been hacked giving him that time to manoeuvre himself next to the building he needed. He had timed himself on runs to make sure he was fast enough to make it in the set time he had given himself. To him, that was another crucial element of any mission or job he had done. The small details were the important difference between success and failure. No matter what the end result was, if he hadn't included and considered every little detail, it was a failure to him. He would not miss out anything, even though he knew the no plan ever survived first contact, he was confident in his abilities to adapt. But so far, so good. He would need to cover the ground in the time he had set himself and onto the next part. He knew that this part was slightly easier as he was concealed from an element of exposure but inside a building was a whole different ball game.

He made his way towards the outer building door and knew that he had to get past the security measures, but he had been assured that the hack had been completed without compromising him. Only now would that be truly tested.

As he positioned himself next to the door, he put all his faith in James and his team that they had been successful in hacking into their systems and over rode each part, only now will he know. He placed a finger onto his throat mic and clicked it "James, do you hear me?" He said in a low voice. He waited a moment or two "I'm here Ronin, I can hear you loud and clear, I can see that you're at the door, you'll need a code to bypass it, key in ZX9521 and then A and you'll be in, over" Ronin looked at the keypad which had a faint glow through his goggles. He pressed each digit slowly Z X 9 5 2 1 and then A. Nothing. He tried again, still nothing. Something was worrying him as he tilted his head to his right and could sense movement. He quickly pressed on his throat mic again, "James, it's not working and Yamada's guards are getting pretty close to home, I have less than four minutes and they'll be on top of me" he said. Another pause and James replied "We've hacked into the central system, they've changed the code again, it seems to be on a cycle. Try ZX765 and then A, that should work"

Ronin pressed each digit carefully but he was getting more anxious that every passing moment would bring Yamada's guards that much closer. He pressed the final A and there was a click just as he heard the faint down step of a foot about fifty metres away from him. He pulled on the door handle and the door opened, as he cracked it open, a dim light was emulating from a passageway. He stepped through the doorway. He looked ahead and saw no movement ahead. He pulled the door to as he stepped into the passageway. There was enough darkness to use his NVG's which would give him an advantage. He could move quickly in the darkness. He had spent enough time over his life doing it. For a moment he wasn't within Yamada's building but back in a small compound, dark and only his senses to guide him. His hands and feet were the only sensory guides he had as he moved forward making his way through what seemed like a maze. The voice of his instructor spoke loud within him "Once you become one with the darkness, to make peace with it, will you be able to manipulate it, make it your friend instead of your enemy. Trust in your instincts and they will guide you" and then he was back in the moment, in Yamada's building and he knew that those words were as true now as they ever were.

CHAPTER FORTY-EIGHT

"Guide me James, where next?" Said Ronin as he made his way forward. The building had that cold feeling to it but not enough to affect Ronin. The passageway was longer than he had thought, even though he had seen the building in a 3D model. He had memorised enough of it to get a general understanding of it. He knew the only direction he needed was up one floor and along another passageway to reach the possible location of Sakai. This was exactly why he was here, that was his only purpose. He knew Yamada needed to be stopped but if he had the opportunity to do that then he would take it, but that wasn't his priority at this moment.

"You need to keep moving forward another ten foot and you will come to a doorway, there's another keypad you'll need to bypass but that's been hacked into already, same as the internal cameras, we've managed to loop it so all they'll see is a delay of a minute and previous footage. That's the best we can offer you so you'll have to move quick. Once you get up to the next level via that stairwell, there are roaming patrols consisting of about two patrols every twenty minutes, so you're safe. I have the keypad code for the next door, ZX451 and then B, that'll get you through" James explained. It was never going to be all this easy Ronin thought as he approached the doorway.

He pressed the keypad in the correct order and the door opened. He slowly opened the door and made his way through. He had arrived at the bottom of a stairwell which when he looked up, he could see that it went up pretty far. He made his way up the outer side of the stairs, staying against the wall moving quickly. As he approached the first level he stopped, there was something wrong, he just knew it. He crouched there waiting and watching but he did not want to use voice coms or that would change everything. He knew that Sakai was being held on the second floor but there was one guard positioned next to the first level doorway. There was no way he could get past them without warning the rest of the building. He considered all the choices he had and all of them were that of action. He slowly placed his foot on the next step and lifted himself up just enough to see ahead of him. There stood a figure but he could clearly see that he was armed with a rifle. He knew from experience that it would take around less than five seconds for someone to lift their weapon into the shoulder and be aiming at their target ahead.

He cycled through all his options again and decided that a diversionary tactic would work as he slipped his hand into a pouch by his waist and pulled out some small ball bearings, these were heavy enough to create an element of noise but not enough to travel. Also, he removed a small catapult that he now had aimed at the stairwell rail on the second floor. But he would have to be careful as this could be two guards he would need to deal with, that was a risk he would have to deal with. That way he could create a sound that came from that way. He pulled back further on the elastic and released the cup as the ball sailed through the air and hitting the rail above his head with a ping when it deflected off the rail. In that same instance, the guard moved forward and then Ronin struck. He moved quick, within less than five seconds he had reached the guard and slipped an arm around his throat, and then his other arm until it cupped the back of his head until he had him in a rear naked choke. He tightened his grip until the guard slumped, which allowed Ronin to drop him low enough to position him against the wall. He knew he would regain consciousness in time so he would need to act fast but at least he knew there wasn't a second guard on the floor above. The only choice he had was to remove the magazine from his rifle as well as the spare ones in his pouch. That way, he may have his rifle but no ammunition to use. He stored them within a side pouch until he could dispose of them somewhere. He reached up and pressed on his throat mic "James, I've just had to neutralise one of the guards on the first floor, I haven't got long so I need code for the second floor and to hack into the camera system to loop the footage" he said. "You need ZX682 and then D Ronin, camera's are on a time delay loop and so far there seems to be only one more guard patrolling on the second floor close to where Sakai is being held" replied James. Ronin decided that it would be better to limit the guards ability to move, so he pulled out a couple of plastic tie wraps and moved the guard down until he was laying on the floor, positioned him with his arms behind his back and tightened the tie wraps around his wrists, next he used some thick gaffer tape he kept with him to seal his mouth the best he could do. Once he was secure he took a few calming breaths to reduce the amount of adrenaline that had been dumped into his system and moved quickly up the next stairwell until he reached the next floor. He kept low and made his way to the next door and pressed the combination onto the keypad. Now was the time to move as he pulled open the door.

CHAPTER FORTY-NINE

The dim lighting of the passageway allowed Ronin to focus upon what was happening. There was no guards present but he knew that they would be there somewhere. He remembered that the location of Sakai was a few doors down but he needed an exact location to be sure. He pressed his throat mic "Which one is it James?" He asked and awaited an answer. It took a moment but he got the reply he needed "Third door down Ronin, but be mindful that we're seeing movement near the end of the passageway, not sure if you can make anything out but there is definitely someone there. The door code is ZX941 and then S, you'll have to be quick" He replied.

Ronin made a quick scan of the passageway and decided that there was no better time than now as he swiftly made his way down towards the door. As he reached it, he stopped and made sure that it was all clear as he turned and pressed the combination. All he wanted was to get Sakai out of there safely. For some reason he was getting a feeling that something wasn't right but he had to push that back as he pressed the last S and allowed the lock to disengage. He pushed the door and looked within, he suddenly wished he had used his NVG's to scan the room to make sure as what was ahead of him wasn't what he had expected.

There was no sign of Sakai but then his world erupted into chaos. There stood several armed men pointing guns in his direction, it was a trap, as the lights came on and a bank of screens on the left hand side of the room lit up.

There was Yamada standing in a larger room next to Sakai who was seated. He looked directly at Ronin and spoke "Bailey-san, you've done well but your team didn't take into account that the motion sensors we have built in have been monitoring your every move, same as the cameras that they did not expect which were linked to an entirely different network have been capturing your every movement. Quite a show so far I must admit, but now it ends. All I propose is that you join me and hand over the sword of Hanzō and you and Sakai can walk out of here free men, no further action will be taken. My men will escort you to me, but believe me, if you try any kind of action they have been given orders to stop you whatever way they can, do you agree with that?" He said.

Ronin knew he was outnumbered and the fire-power that was presented towards him, he wouldn't have much chance of shifting the balance of a victory. He knew he would have to create a new plan and allow Yamada to believe he had victory for this time. He looked at the screen and replied "Yes Yamada-san, I agree to your terms, as long as there is no further action taken" Yamada shook his head in agreement and simply replied "Good, I look forward to seeing you soon, my men will escort you to me"

Ronin's mind was filled with various scenarios but for now he had to shut them all out and concentrate on the very moment as Yamada's men stepped forward, a couple of them walked past him and stopped whilst the others were behind him, one of them pointed towards the doorway. Ronin turned and followed the men in front of him, he knew if he was quick he could easily have taken out a couple of them but his fight wasn't with them, it was with Yamada, so he decided that he would concentrate on that moment instead. As they made their way along the passageway and through another doorway, it led into a large room. Very exquisitely decorated in a Japanese style. It was lined around the edges with tatami mats and in the centre of the room was Sakai seated upon a chair with Yamada behind him. They both looked up as Ronin entered the room.

"Welcome Bailey-san, please join us, we have a lot to discuss"

CHAPTER FIFTY

As Ronin looked ahead of him, he looked at both Sakai and Yamada, but he was taking in his surroundings at the same time. He realised to fight his way out of this situation, he would have a fight on his hands and although he could handle most that was presented to him, it wouldn't be possible to do this himself. Yamada stood behind Sakai smartly dressed in a dark grey suit, surrounded by at least fifteen armed bodyguards, weapons in a relaxed position but ones that Ronin knew that would be brought to firing positions at any given moment. His only way out of this was possible to talk it but even that he would have to play his hand well.

Yamada stepped forward and spoke "Bailey-san, let's cut to the chase right now. You and I have been searching for the elusive sword of Hanzō, which I see you have been more successful than myself. I know you think that you believe that you're doing the people of Japan a service to bring the sword back to them, but we both know the power that it holds. I know that this isn't something that can be kept in a museum and locked behind glass for thousands of people to stare at. So I propose that you hand it over and I can find a better purpose for it than any museum can use it for" he said. Ronin knew that was a lie and knew exactly what Yamada's true intentions were and they were not wholesome. If he held the sword now, he would use it for his own gain, to hold a power over the people like a Shogun. He needed to persuade him and keep hood of it. How he was going to do this was something he was working on.

Ronin looked at Yamada and before he spoke looked at Sakai with a look that said more than he could ever say. "Yamada-san, you and I know that the sword truly belongs to the people of Japan. This was Hanzō true intention, for it to be used for the good, to unite them as one rather than divide them. If you hold it, we both know the power you would have over them. I could have easily thrown the separated pieces into different oceans, for them to be gone forever. But I didn't, for one single reason. They belong to the people of Japan and they decide what is done with it. No amount of money can ever buy this neither will it be any better being held by yourself, so let's be honest here. If I was to hand it over, which I easily could and all this would be over for myself and Sakai. To walk out of here, which I know isn't really a reality either. I know that you would simply hold a power over your enemies which would simply allow you to gain more wealth than possible. So why don't we propose a deal?" He said.

Yamada looked at Ronin, trying to work out his intentions but it was difficult to see as he was clouded by one purpose and that was to gain hold of the sword. He knew he could simply command his men to remove it by force but that was too easy, so he decided to hear him out. "And what would that be Bailey-san? What could you propose that would change this situation into something that would both see us walk away from this with a peaceful deal" he asked.

Ronin had kept his cards close to his chest for some time, but there was one thing that he knew Yamada wouldn't back down so easily. "You've heard of the blade of a thousand cuts and that it can slice through the toughest of materials. Isn't this how Hanzō beat his enemies? He simply cut right through them, even the toughest material couldn't stop it. Now not many people have heard of it but Graphene is quite possibly one of the strongest materials known to man. Even one atom-thick sheets of carbon are 200 times stronger than steel. It has been said that it would take an elephant balancing on a pencil to break a sheet as thin as Saran wrap. So whilst we could quite easily propose a test of olden days which includes cutting through bamboo. Let's see if our skills with the blade can see best each other with seeing who can make a clean cut through it. But not just one sheet but three? Whoever can, walks away"

Yamada looked at Ronin, slightly bemused with this arrogance against him but wouldn't allow him to see that he had proposed a deal that even he hadn't thought of. He mused over the idea a couple of moments and then replied "I agree Bailey-san, let us sit and have some tea whilst we wait for the materials to be gathered, we both know where there this amount is stored. You've bought yourself some time at least"

Ronin knew that Yamada in fact did have a small storage of Graphene and that it wouldn't take long for it to be gathered. He at least time for now until the next part of his plan to fall into place.

CHAPTER FIFTY-ONE

They sat concentrating on the steam gently rising from the cups, small whispers of steam dancing in the air around the cups as they consumed the green tea. Ronins mind was cycling through the multiple options as he shifted his fingers on the small cup. He watched as a couple of men brought in the stand and started to assemble the structure, placing the graphene sheets onto it. Such thin plates they looked as each one was fitted into place upon it. His thoughts started to drift back to the time when he was stood in front of the bamboo poles, sword in hand. It was always the ultimate test of any swordsman's skills.

This practice had a name and it was simply known as Tameshigiri. It is an art form that focuses on performing cutting tests with a Japanese sword against an object, usually tatami in the cleanest and most elegant way possible. It is a practice that's hundreds of years old, initially used by samurai to test the edge of their Katana sword.

Japanese martial arts with swords like Kendo and Iaido practice are those that use it, even in modern times, it has built a culture around it. In modern times, the practice of *tameshigiri* has come to focus on testing the swordsman's abilities, rather than the sword's own abilities. The swords used are typically inexpensive ones so not to damage the blades. Practitioners of *tameshigiri* sometimes use the terms *Shito* 試刀 which is known as sword testing as well as *Shizan* 試斬 which is known as test cutting, an alternate pronunciation of the characters for *tameshigiri*. This is to distinguish between the historical practice of testing swords and the contemporary practice of testing one's cutting ability. The target most often used is the tatami 'Omote' rush mat. To be able to cut consecutive times on one target, or to cut multiple targets while moving, this requires that they are to be very skilled swordsman.

Targets today are typically made from *goza*, which is the top layer of the traditional tatami floor covering, it is either bundled or rolled into a cylindrical shape. They may be soaked in water to add density to the material. This density is to represent that of flesh. Green bamboo is used to represent bone.

Once the *goza* target is in this cylindrical shape, it has a vertical grain pattern when stood vertically on a target stand, or horizontally when placed on a horizontal target stand *which is known as dotton* or *dodan*. This direction of the grain affects the difficulty of the cut.

The difficulty of cuts is a combination of the target material hardness, the direction of the grain of the target of there is any, the quality of the sword, the angle of the blade which is known as hasuji, on impact, and the angle of the swing of the sword *which is known as tachsuji.*

When cutting a straw target that is standing vertically, swordsmen found that the easiest cut is the downward diagonal. This is due to a combination of the angle of impact of the cut against the grain which is approximately 30-50 degrees from the surface, the downward diagonal angle of the swing, and the ability to use many of the major muscle groups and rotation of the body to aid in the cut.

Next in difficulty was to be found in the upward diagonal cut which has the same angle, but works against gravity and uses slightly different muscles and rotation. The third in difficulty is the straight downward cut, not in terms of the grain but in terms of the group of muscles involved. The most difficult cut of the four basic cuts is the horizontal direction (against a vertical target) as it is directly perpendicular to the grain of the target.

Ronin had practiced multiple times against smaller setups with one to two bamboo poles, cutting and repeating the practice until he got it right. An additional pole was added and he would start again. His muscles would scream after practicing several hours, but he knew that he would regain the muscle memory after many attempts. The repetition of this practice honed his skill until he could cut through multiple poles. He began to see it as a form of meditation, concentrating on his posture and breathing.

His memories were disturbed by the placement of a pole upon the stand. He refocused as he saw a single steel pole being lowered into place, this would be the first test pole and a fairly easy one at any given moment, but the material would be the greatest of tests. Ronin knew that there was only one sword that was capable of cutting through all four poles and he was carrying it with him upon his back.

He looked directly at Yamada and knew that it would soon be time, he couldn't allow him to know that the blade he was carrying was the one that Yamada was willing to kill for. He knew that he could at least buy himself enough time whilst he could consider what he would do next. There was six heavily armed men in the room and even as fast as he was, that would be testing him to his limits, and then there was Yamada himself. He knew that he was indeed a skilled swordsman in himself and won many fights with Shinai which is the bamboo sword used in Kendo, which Yamada himself was highly competent in.

Once that first pole was firmly fixed into place, Yamada stood. He looked upon Ronin, a slight arrogance within his facial expression and said "Shall we begin Bailey-san?"

CHAPTER FIFTY-TWO

Yamada stood relaxed, knees bent.

He looked at Ronin and simply said "I am ready Bailey-san, shall we begin, let's see the truth of any of this whether the blade of Hanzō truly is as strong as it is claimed to be shall we?"

Ronin knew this was it, if he sprung forward to attack Yamada, that would be classed as cowardly as he was unarmed and he would be cut down. He knew that he had no choice. He reached up and over his shoulder and unclipped Hanzō's sword, drew it out and then stood, the blade lay perfectly balanced horizontally. He stepped forward until he was standing directly in front of Yamada, the blade of the Katana was facing him as tradition dictated as he held it up to Yamada before bowing. Yamada gave a bow and accepted with both hands whilst keeping perfect eye alignment with each other, not one giving anything away to the other. He positioned himself in a very traditional stance that was called Chūdan-no-kamae, which is known as the middle posture.

This is the most basic stance, it allows for a balance between attacking and defensive postures. When it's performed correctly, the practitioner's trunk and right wrist are protected. All students learn this posture first, so they know the correct striking distance.

Whilst stood within the chūdan-no-kamae posture, Yamada's left foot was a few inches behind his right foot, he kept his left heel elevated. His hips remained forward and his shoulders were relaxed as he concentrated on the pole in front of him. It would be an easy cut, one he had practiced thousands of times, he did not think of the pole in front of him as Graphene but just the standard bamboo. He simply couldn't believe that he was possibly holding the very sword that Hanzō had all that time ago as he defeated his enemies, very much as he would Ronin. He would show him that he was a greater swordsman, he knew this way he would defeat Ronin whilst a duel would be evenly matched.

He looked directly at the pole whilst slightly adjusting his stance, it would be the best of three cuts with three rolled Graphene poles, one would be usually a healthy competition but three. That would be extremely challenging. He would lift and shift himself slightly to his right as he lifted the sword to create a diagonal cut, as he angled the blade. He took several deep breaths before he performed a Kiai which is a Japanese term used in martial arts, for the short shout uttered when performing an attacking move. This explosive energy radiated through him and cut right through the pole. Yamada felt good using the blade, he wasn't sure but he definitely felt different using it.

One of his men moved forward and removed the cut pole whilst another two moved forward with a pole each and fitted them onto the stand, ready for Yamada to take his second cut. This time he chose to use the Jōdan-no-kamae, which is the high posture used in kenjutsu. This stance involves keeping your sword raised above your head, with the tip of the blade pointed back. As there are actually different styles of jōdan-no-kamae, one involves keeping your left foot in front, while the other involves holding the sword with a single hand, the former of which is usually the most popular style in kenjutsu. This was the stance that Yamada chose to use as he positioned himself slightly wider than usual but keeping light in his stance. He would use a powerful downwards diagonal cut to slice through the pole. This would be his choice of cuts for the next two.

He focused upon the pole before releasing a powerful explosion of Kiai energy and cut through both of the poles, although there was a lot more resistance this time and it could be clearly seen in Yamada's facial expression as a bead of sweat appeared upon his forehead.

Ronin could tell that Yamada was tiring through his expression. He looked upon Yamada and could see that the next cut would push him to the very limit of his abilities as he stood waiting for the next set of poles to be set up. A couple of Yamada's men brought forward three poles and fitted them together whilst Yamada stood and then raised the sword back into the Jōdan-no-kamae posture. He was taking several deep breaths followed by concentrated exhales. He fully fell into this cycle of breaths until he reached the last limit and refocused whilst he gripped the Tsuka. His voice then exploded in a loud exhale of Kiai as he brought down the sword in a fast motion as it passed through the first two poles cleanly, as it reached the last couple of millimetres of the last pole, it halted, no further it passed through and Yamada slumped as his grip relaxed.

His rear leg dropped down as his head lowered. He was done, he could not hold his body within a relaxed position and dropped down as a couple of his men moved forward and steadied him. The room was silent. Yamada was the first to speak "Well, I have been bested by the blade of a thousand cuts, or should I say, the poles became a wall that I could not penetrate. I believe it is your attempt Bailey-san" he said as he looked at Ronin with a pained expression. He had been defeated by the third pole.

CHAPTER FIFTY-THREE

R onin stepped forward and stopped before Yamada. One of his men had removed the sword that was lodged within the third pole and as tradition dictated, he handed over the sword with the blade facing himself to show that he had no bad intentions towards Ronin. Both men bowed out of respect and Ronin gripped the swords Tsuka but something felt different. It was if all the energy in the world was flowing through it and into him. He switched off from these emotions as he positioned himself whilst Yamada's men prepared the first pole. Yamada himself had been helped by his men and seated whilst they passed water over to him. He spoke slowly and quieter than usual "In your own time Bailey-san, as your aware, if you cut through all three then you have won this competition and beaten me, are you ready" he asked.

Ronin stood relaxed within the Chūdan-no-kamae position and nodded after Yamada had spoken. He was mentally preparing himself which flowed through him physically. He raised the sword and let it flow diagonally downwards in a short burst of concentrated energy which saw the blade cleanly cut through the pole. Ronin allowed himself to take several cleansing breaths as Yamada's men prepared the next set of poles whilst Ronin positioned himself with the Jōdan-no-kamae position. He took several deep breaths whilst he completed this cycle. His mind was focused upon one thing and that was past the point which the blade would pass the second pole. He disconnected his mind from the external world and inwardly travelled as he found himself reminiscing in past times whilst he remembered standing in his first time of cutting bamboo poles and his Sensei's calming voice flowing through him.

"Don't think of it as a solid object, allow it to pass through it like it is water, feel the resistance but don't fool yourself into thinking it is impossible. Once you feel the passage of air around it change, only then will you know that you are ready"

The voice faded away as he refocused and let out a powerful Kiai. The blade cleanly sliced through both poles as though they were water, he could feel the resistance but strangely enough it was as if the sword itself was energising him. He had never felt anything like that before. He allowed himself to oxygenate his body as Yamada's men removed the two cut poles and prepared the final three. This was it and Ronin knew it. Yamada was looking upon him, slightly bemused but in some way blank as if he was trying to work out what level of discomfort was he in right now.

Ronin blocked that out as he prepared himself for the final test. He was allowing the cycle of breaths to cleanse him as he raised the sword once more. He refocused and then it happened, his mind exploded into thousands of small thoughts but through it, he could see himself standing there by the blade had cleanly passed through the three poles. He shut out all thoughts as he hit a peak, it was as if he was atop Mount Fuji itself as a bird and tilted down flying down towards the base in an explosive path of energy that flowed through him as the blade travelled its own path. It passed through the first, second and then everyone in that room watched its trajectory in absolute silence and apprehension.

Even Yamada himself had shifted forward as he sat waiting and watching as the blade continued on and finally reached its destination. Past the third. Ronin had done it, he had cut through three poles. He didn't know what to say as he sat watching Ronin's chest heave with deepening breaths and then relax fully, his body slumping and then steadying himself.

Ronin let his body relax as he stood tall, he gripped the Tsuba and could still feel the power pulsating through it. He couldn't believe that he had done it. He looked upon Yamada, who sat silent, his whole body had slumped in a way that anyone that had experienced defeat could do. The silence in the room was broken by Yamada himself "Congratulations Bailey-san, quite an impressive display of skill and strength. I didn't think that you would have done it but you're a better man than myself I admit that but to allow you to leave here without seeing another display of your skills would be a failure on my part" he said.

Ronin was surprised but not entirely as this was Yamada he was talking to. He awaited for what he had lined up for him. He scanned the room, there was fifteen armed guards and two doorways, so he would need to fight through all fifteen and then get past the rest of the security measures to get out of here. Plus the rest of Yamada's security team. That was quite a task. He knew that the chances of Sakai and himself getting out of here without some kind of fight was minimal. He looked at Yamada and spoke "What would you suggest Yamada-san? Haven't I earned the right for myself and Sakai-san to leave? I've beaten you in one contest of skill, what have you got planned if I can ask?"

Yamada was quiet for a moment and then it was as if Ronin had been sucker punched, taken completely by surprised when Yamada spoke next. "Please step forward Higanbana, as you're aware Bailey-san, there's always been rumours of a person that I employ who is one of my personal guards that everyone fears. So I like to present them myself and I'm sure you know them well" he said as Higanbana themselves stepped forward into the light.

It was as if Ronin had been hit by a tsunami, all his thoughts came crashing down on him at once, but kept his composure the best he could as he spoke their name "Emiko"

CHAPTER FIFTY-FOUR

E miko stepped forward and looked at Ronin. The look upon his face said it all and she knew in that instance that this was it. The moment that she had almost broken his spirit. She wasn't sure what she was going to say, all this time that she had to think about the words she would say, the excuses she would use to justify herself and yet they wouldn't come. She took a deep breath and looked upon Ronin.

"Brother, I know what you're thinking and believe me, I didn't want this moment to come either. I've never wanted you to be put in this situation. There's so much I want to say but I know that it won't change anything. Let's just say that father made a few deals with Yamada before he died and yet I was part of those. My contract with Yamada is still valid and although even though when father died, I tried to break it but a deal is a deal and some contracts can't be broken by money. For you and Sakai-san to walk out of here alive with Hanzō's sword was never going to happen and Yamada knew that. He knew that by targeting Sakai-san and threatening him with what he would do to his family would break him. I also knew that you wouldn't allow Sakai-san to be left to suffer like this. So I decided to create my own deal. Whoever wins this fight, walks away free. Either me from my contract or you and Sakai-san with Hanzō's sword. That's the best deal I could broker with Yamada-san. So what's it going to be brother?"

Ronin was silent, more silent than he had ever been in his life. He knew the decision that he would make next would change everything. He didn't want to fight Emiko yet he wanted to see at least Sakai leave here to return to his family. He knew the only way they all would leave here was to see the end of Yamada himself. His death would end all contracts, not only Emiko's but also his security team. If Yamada died here tonight then it would be over. He thought he had drawn a good hand but that wasn't to be. He knew he had one last trick before he either left here alive or carried out to be laid upon a pyre.

Ronin stood there in mid thought and breathed a deep and calming breath before looking at both Yamada and Emiko. If death was going to visit then today it wasn't going to be him and he was going to make sure of it. He stepped forward, sword in hand and walked into the centre of the room. He stopped and simply said "So let it be" as he raised the sword into the Chūdan-no-kamae position. He knew that this was the position that would win his battle ahead of him since Emiko favoured Jōdan-no-kamae but decided to start with Chūdan-no-kamae. This would be the dance to end all dances as they looked at each other. As Musashi famously quoted 'Whoever flinches first loses' and Ronin knew that it wouldn't be himself. He lunged forward whilst Emiko brought herself into a defensive position. The lunges and parries continued, circling each other trying to break each other's defences. There were a few clashes of the blade until Ronin decided to test Emiko's external defences as he stepped forward and lifted the sword before he changed positions and swiftly brought the sword across her body horizontally and back into Waki-gamae which involved hiding his sword behind his body, exposing only the sword's pommel to Emiko, but also allowing him to bring it up in a powerful uppercut motion which Emiko quickly changed position to defend, but Ronin knew what she was going to do, mid cut he shifted and drew his sword and body backwards to bring it up into the Jōdan-no-kamae position and just as Ronin was going to execute his final cut, he could feel the power needed to break the blade coarse through his body. It was if the heaven and earth had met as he brought it down upon Emiko's sword in one final blow as it went right through it and almost into the floor below but Ronin stopped before impact.

Silence entered the room as both of them stood, their bodies wracked with deep breaths as they concentrated on regaining their posture and breath. Emiko's shattered blade was still within her hand which she was looking at whilst the rest lay upon the floor. Ronin knew that Yamada wouldn't allow them to leave, he knew that he would react to this defeat and he was fully prepared to meet his redemption.

CHAPTER FIFTY-FIVE

Yamada went to stand and then it happened, Ronin flinched as he saw flashes in his mind of what was to be, he had woken many times with this image in his mind's eye, he never knew who the shadow was but he knew that this was now, and the shadow was forming into what was drawing themselves up to step forward. He twisted his wrist slightly, allowing his hand to bring the sword at the right angle as he released his left hand allowing the full swing to proceed whilst shifting his right foot sideways. He knew the angle was correct as he felt the surge of energy through him as he released the Tsuka from his right hand and let if fly like an eagle towards its prey. It flew true and penetrated Yamada's body and continued to on its trajectory until it sliced itself way through sinew, flesh and finally leather and wood until the Tsuba slammed against flesh and bone pinning Yamada's body in place.

The room fell silent as they all looked at Yamada who slumped in his chair knowing that he was inhaling his final breath. He looked up at Ronin and spoke in a quiet voice "You've finally done what was needed to be done then. I didn't think you had what it took, but now I can see that you are what was said about you all this time and you've found the redemption to end all that is within. You've made the decision needed to end this. You know you'll never make it out of here" he said with his final breath as he slumped forward and lay still.

In that moment Ronin knew that it was either fight or flight but he had bigger problems to deal with. There was still Yamada's men to deal with but as he prepared to fight his way out of the room he could see one of the men step forward and lift his weapon. Sakai knew he could reach him if he moved now but as he did, they lifted their helmet and pulled down their face mask to reveal themselves. "Let's get out of here Ronin" they said as he stopped in his tracks especially as they didn't address him in typical Japanese style. Only those of western culture would do that.

Ronin wasn't even sure at first what to do but he switched off to everything that he was originally thinking as the man stepped forward and revealed himself. "What the hell are you doing here Brett?" He asked, still confused to what was happening.

Brett hadn't aged since the last time he had seen him in the Station Hotel with the details of the job that started all this. He was still trying to get his head around it all when Brett spoke "Well I was tasked on another job when Kenji contacted me, he asked me as a favour to step in when he told me about what happened buddy, I knew of a few guys on Yamada's security detail and got in on the task. I knew you could handle yourself but something bugged me that maybe you had taken on something bigger than all of us. So what's next?" He asked. Ronin wasn't sure what to even say at first as he stood looking around. Sakai and Emiko were there and he was still alive so at least that was an advantage.

He looked at them and knew what the answer was going to be as he walked over to where Yamada was still slumped in his chair. He reached out and placed his hand over the Tsuka and pulled whilst he positioned his hand upon Yamada. The sword withdrew itself, blood smeared upon it. He looked around and said "You got any water?" As he looked at Brett. "We need to get this cleaned up and prepared to be handed back over to who it truly belongs to, the people of Japan. No one shall ever hold it again and it shall be sealed back within Hanzō's tomb beneath Sainen-Ji. This is over and at least no one can unleash its power again. I felt what it was capable of and I was scared of it. You know me, fear never enters my mind but this time, I knew it was real. If it is left in open display then someone will always create an opportunity to use for the worst reasons and we can't let that happen" He explained as he stood looking at all those around him. "Let's return it home, back where it belongs to its true master"

CHAPTER FIFTY-SIX

The darkened passage was lit by the head torches of both Ronin and Sakai as they stood in front of the partial shrine that existed beneath the earth. As Ronin placed the sword within the lacquered box and then closed it, he felt the last of the energy flowing from his hands as he brought them together to pray, he whispered deeply;

"Mi wa tatoi
Musashi no nobe ni
Kuchinu tomo
Todome okamashi
Yamato damashii"

(Even if my body
decays on the fields of Musashi,
my Japanese soul
will live forever)

The words he spoke were the famous Haiku written by Yoshida Shoin who was executed 1859 for his part in a plot to asssinate a shogunate official. He was a complicated young man, he was a patriot, scholar, terrorist and beloved teacher to students, who later led the Meiji Restoration. But they resonated with him in this moment.

They both stood and silently made their way back about five metres from the entrance of the tomb. Ronin looked at Sakai and spoke softly "You do know if we seal this chamber, then it would take an army of miners to retrieve the sword again Sakai-san"

Sakai knew of the consequences of their actions but he knew it was for the best, he looked at Ronin and replied "It's for the best Bailey-san. The power that sword holds is far too much for anyone, you've felt it and even though it is here now in its resting place, when will the next person come along who will seek it for bad intentions? We can't allow that to happen and see any destruction happen, let us get this done and return back to our lives"

Ronin knew this was the right course of action, they had returned it to the people of Japan and it's rightful resting place. He lifted the detonator and spoke the words he had said in those final moments with his own father "Yama to shite no gimu wa omoiga, shi wa hane yori mo karui" (Duty is heavy as a mountain but Death is lighter than a feather) and pressed the button. The passageway was quickly filled with dust and earth as it fell inwardly, filling the void. Silence fell and they were left with no more words as they turned around and made their way to the surface. They both knew that they had done the right thing and their souls felt a little lighter as they walked.

"So what now" asked Emiko as they stood by the entrance of Sainen-Ji whilst the sun set on a cool evening. Ronin took a few moments before he answered but he knew what he was going to say, whether he found the right words were a different matter.

"We've all come together, battled through adversity and conquered the moment. What comes next is not for us to decide but fate itself. I may have found redemption for all that's passed, but I shall time at the Joruri-ji garden. For I know that the bells that ring will be my reminder that there is still evil within this world and although we can never be truly free from its existence, we can take action that keeps it at bay in the best way we can. Now let's enjoy what's left of this evening. For tomorrow can wait, tonight we celebrate life with this family that we are"

REDEMPTION

The sun was slowly setting over the Joruri-ji garden, it's glow touched upon every part of it. Especially the great Bonshō bells, which Ronin was kneeling by. He was touching out onto the world through his mind as concentrated on his breath and yet he knew he was more connected to the moment than he cared to admit to.

"So what's next brother?" Asked a voice behind him. He slowly brought himself back into this world, allowing himself to find his mind returning to a place where reality fought with the true consciousness of humanity around him. He knew that Emiko had been standing there for a while, but he allowed himself to dissociate himself from the moment.

He opened his eyes and released his final exhale and answered. "To be honest with you sister, I know this journey is soon to come to an end. I can no longer keep walking down this path. I've been fighting against my soul for a long time and I know that all I wanted was to know that all that I've done was for a reason, to make an impact upon the world around me. I can't change all that I've done but I can let it all go. I'm financially independent where money can't dictate my direction. For this was never about money or ego but using my skills to change unchangeable situations for the better. For I know I've struggled for a long time with the question of why me? Why was I born with these abilities? Why, why, why I keep asking myself but I know the answer isn't mine alone. For I know we're all born with the ability to change the world in some way, for better or worse, that's all we can control. I can't explain how I do it, but I know I can use to make tomorrow easier to live for others. I fear inside that I've picked up the sword for one last time, but I also feel that the next time I pick it up, it'll be my last. I live by the sword but do I really want to die by it? Well I guess fate will decide that outcome. I can't stay here within this moment forever. You're free sister and you have a life ahead of you, Higanbana can never have a hold over you again, let it die. For we all need to sacrifice a part of our soul to find the peace needed to exist within a world that we don't have much control over our destiny. We think we do but it's all an illusion. Go live for me and when the gods have finished with me, I'll join you, but remember I'll always stand by you. That's never going to change, you're never going to be alone again and if time could be wheeled back again, I would always enter that building to get you out, just remember that"

Emiko stood silent at first, but thought that she had nothing to lose "Be at peace brother, you deserve that at least, you have nothing more to prove. The world needs more people like you, the ones prepared to claim a little bit of redemption for all they have done, but how many are willing to burn their souls to set fire to the night to see the dawn rise the next day? We'll never know but I know you can sleep deep and rest well"

Ronin had not much to say after that but he knew the winds of change had happened and he was quite happy to glide upon its breath. "I love you too sister, I have rang the bells of redemption for the last time, for the next time we'll be on the other side and that's something that life can't change, but as tomorrow isn't promised, let's live for today"

Printed in Great Britain
by Amazon